P9-DOG-962

PRAISE FOR THE **TRACK** SERIES

"Reynolds has created a character whose journey is so
genuine that he's worthy of a place alongside Ramona
and Joey Pigza on the bookshelves where our most
beloved, imperfect characters live."
—*New York Times* on *Ghost*

★"This is raw and lyrical, and as funny as it is
heartbreaking. . . . An absolute must-read for anyone
who has ever wondered how fast you must be to run
away from yourself."
—*Booklist*, starred review of *Ghost*

★"The story of Ghost's evolving relationships with his
anger, with his ever-worried mother, with Coach Brody,
and with running is a joy to read."
—*Shelf Awareness*, starred review of *Ghost*

★"Compulsively readable . . . Another literary pacesetter
that will leave Reynolds's readers wanting more."
—*Kirkus Reviews*, starred review of *Sunny*

★"Reynolds again uses his entrancing grasp of voice to
pull readers into the heartbreaking world of the
Track series."
—*Booklist*, starred review of *Sunny*

also by **jason reynolds**

When I Was the Greatest

The Boy in the Black Suit

All American Boys

As Brave As You

Ghost

Long Way Down

Sunny

For Every One

Lu

PATINA

TRACK: BOOK 2

jason **reynolds**

A Caitlyn Dlouhy Book

ATHENEUM BOOKS FOR YOUNG READERS
New York London Toronto Sydney New Delhi

If you purchased this book without a cover, you should be aware that this book is stolen property. It was reported as "unsold and destroyed" to the publisher, and neither the author nor the publisher has received any payment for this "stripped book."

ATHENEUM BOOKS FOR YOUNG READERS
An imprint of Simon & Schuster Children's Publishing Division
1230 Avenue of the Americas, New York, New York 10020
This book is a work of fiction. Any references to historical events, real people, or real places are used fictitiously. Other names, characters, places, and events are products of the author's imagination, and any resemblance to actual events or places or persons, living or dead, is entirely coincidental.
Text copyright © 2017 by Jason Reynolds
Cover illustrations copyright © 2017 by Vanessa Brantley-Newton
All rights reserved, including the right of reproduction in whole or in part in any form.
ATHENEUM BOOKS FOR YOUNG READERS is a registered trademark of Simon & Schuster, Inc. Atheneum logo is a trademark of Simon & Schuster, Inc.
For information about special discounts for bulk purchases, please contact Simon & Schuster Special Sales at 1-866-506-1949 or business@simonandschuster.com.
The Simon & Schuster Speakers Bureau can bring authors to your live event. For more information or to book an event, contact the Simon & Schuster Speakers Bureau at 1-866-248-3049 or visit our website at www.simonspeakers.com.
Also available in an Atheneum Books for Young Readers hardcover edition
Book design by Debra Sfetsios-Conover and Irene Metaxatos
The text for this book was set in ITC Stone Serif Std.
Manufactured in the United States of America
1019 OFF
First Atheneum Books for Young Readers paperback edition October 2018
10 9 8 7 6 5
The Library of Congress has cataloged the hardcover edition as follows:
Names: Reynolds, Jason, author.
Title: Patina / Jason Reynolds.
Description: First edition. | New York : Atheneum Books for Young Readers, [2017] | Series: Track ; 2 | "Caitlyn Dlouhy Books." | Summary: "A newbie to the track team, Patina 'Patty' Jones must learn to rely on her family and teammates as she tries to outrun her personal demons."— Provided by publisher.
Identifiers: LCCN 2017018004| ISBN 9781481450188 (hardcover)
ISBN 9781481450195 (paperback) | ISBN 9781481450201 (eBook)
Subjects: | CYAC: Running—Fiction. | Track and field—Fiction. | Stress (Physiology)—Fiction. | Family problems—Fiction. | Diabetes—Fiction. | African Americans—Fiction. | BISAC: JUVENILE FICTION / Sports & Recreation / General. | JUVENILE FICTION / Family / Adoption. | JUVENILE FICTION / Social Issues / Friendship.
Classification: LCC PZ7.R33593 Pat 2017 | DDC [Fic]—dc23
LC record available at https://lccn.loc.gov/2017018004

For those who've been
passed the baton
too young

TO DO: Everything (including forgetting about the race and braiding my sister's hair)

AIN'T NO SUCH thing as a false start. Because false means fake, and ain't no fake starts in track. Either you start or you don't. Either you run or you don't. No in-between. Now, there can be a wrong start. That makes more sense to me. Means you just start at the wrong time. Just jump early and break out running with no one there running with you. No competition except for your own brain that swears there's other people on your heels. But ain't nobody there. Not for real. Ain't no chaser. That's what they really mean when they say false start. A real start at the wrong time.

jason reynolds

And at the first meet of the season, nobody knew this more than Ghost.

Before the race, me and everybody else stood on the sidelines, clapping and hyping Ghost and Lu up as they took their marks. This was of course after they had already gassed each other up, talking to each other like there was no one else on the track but them. Funny how they went from mean-muggin' each other when they first met, to becoming all buddy-buddy like they their own two-man gang or something. Lu and Ghost—sticking together like glue. Ha! Glue! Ghost and Lu, Glue. Get it? That could be their corny crew name. Lost would also work. Matter fact, there was a moment where I thought that name might even be more fitting. Especially after what Ghost did.

See, at first, I thought he'd timed it perfectly. I thought Ghost pushed off from the line at the exact moment the gun went off, as if he just knew when it was coming. Like he could feel it on the inside of him or something. But he didn't hear the second shot. Well, I take that back. Of course he heard it. It was a loud *boom*. It was impossible not to hear it. But he didn't know it meant that he'd jumped too early, that he'd false started. I mean, this was his first race, so he had no clue that that second shot meant to stop running, and start over. So . . . he didn't.

He ran the entire hundred meters. Didn't know that people weren't cheering him on, but were yelling for him to pull up, to go back to the starting line. So when he got to the finish line, he threw his hands up in victory and turned around with one of them million-toothed smiles until he noticed all the other runners—his competition—were still up at the top of the track. He looked out into the crowd. Everybody, laughing. Pointing. Shaking their heads, while Ghost dropped his. Stared at the black tar, his chest like someone blowing up a balloon inside him, then letting the air out, then blowing it back up, then letting the air out. I was afraid that balloon was gonna bust. That Ghost would burst open like he used to do when he first joined the team. And I could tell by the way he was chewing on the side of his jaw that he wanted to, or maybe just keep running, off the track, out of the park, all the way home.

Coach walked over to him, whispered something in his ear. I don't know what it was. But it was probably something like, "It's okay, it's okay, settle down, you're still in it. But if you do it again, you're disqualified." Nah, knowing Coach, it was probably something a little more deep, like . . . I don't know. I can't even think of nothing right now, but Coach was full of deep. Whatever it was, Ghost lifted his head and trotted back to the line, where Lu was waiting with his hand out for a five. Ghost was still out of breath, but there was no time for him to catch it. He had to get back down on his mark. Get ready to run it all over.

The starter held the gun in the air again. My stomach flipped over again. The man pulled the trigger again. *Boom!* again. And Ghost took off. Again. It was almost like his legs were sticks of dynamite, and the first run was just the fuse being lit, and now, the tiny fire had gotten to the blowup part. And let me tell you, Ghost . . . blew up. Busted wide open in the best way. I mean, the dude exploded down the line in a blur, even faster this time, his silver shoes like sparks flicking up off the track.

First race. First place.

Even after a false start.

And if a false start means a real start at the wrong time—the wrong time being too early—then I must've had a false finish, which also ain't a fake finish, but a real finish, just . . . too late. Make sense?

Just in case it don't, let me explain.

My race was up next. And here's the thing, I've been running the eight hundred for three years straight. It's my race. I have a system, a way of running it. I come off the block strong and low and by the time I'm straight up, my stride is steady, but I always allow myself to drop back a little. You know, keeping it cool for the first lap. Pace. That's where eight-hundred runners blow it. They start out too fast and be rigged by the second lap. I seen a lot of girls get roasted out there, showboatin' on that first four hundred. But I knew better. I knew the second four hundred was the kicker. What I didn't know, though, was just how fast the girls in this new league were. What kinda shape they were in. So when the gun blew, and we took off, I realized that the pace I had to keep just to stay with the pack was faster than I was used to. But, of course, I'm thinking, these girls are stupid and are gonna be tired in twenty seconds.

In thirty seconds.

In forty seconds.

Never happened, and instead it ended up being me saying to myself, *Oh God, I'm tired. How am I tired?* And as we rounded into the final two hundred meters, I had to dig deep and step it up. So I turned on the jets.

Here's how it went.

Cornrows, Low-Cut, Ponytail, and Puny-Tail in front of me. *Chop 'em down, Patty. Push, push, push, breathe.* Cornrows is on my side now. The crowd is

5

screaming the traditional chant when someone is getting passed—*Woooop! Woooop! Woooop!* Push. Push. Cornrows is toast. One hundred meters to go. Mouth wide open. Eyes wide open. Stride wide open. Chop 'em down, Patty. Arms pumping, whipping the air out of my way like water. Low-Cut is slowing up. Her little pea-head's bobbling like it could snap right off. She's tired. Finally. *Woooop! Woooop!* Got her. Two more to go. Ponytail can feel me coming. She can probably hear my footsteps over the screaming crowd. She knows I'm close, and then she makes the biggest mistake ever— the one thing every coach tells you to never do—she looked back. See, when you look back, it automatically knocks your stride off and it gets you messed up men- tally. And once Ponytail looked over her shoulder, the *woooops* started back up like a siren. *Woooop! Woooop! Woooop!* Fifty meters. That's right, I'm coming. Chop 'em down, Patty. I'm coming. I could see Puny-Tail just ahead of her, that little twist of hair in the back of her head like a snake tongue. She was running out of breath. I could see that by the way her form had broken down. Ponytail was too. We all were. And even worse for me, we were also running out of track.

I got Ponytail by a nose—second place—then col- lapsed, people cheering all around me, jumping up and down in the stands quickly becoming a wavy blur of color as the tears rose. Second? Stupid second place? Ugh. No way was I going to cry. Trust me, I wanted to, water pricking at my eyelids, but no way. I wanted to kick something, I was so mad! Coach Whit came over and helped me up, and once I was standing, I yanked away from her and limped over to the bench. My legs were burning and cramping, but I wanted to kick something anyway. Maybe kick the bench over. Kick those stupid orange slices Lu's mother brought. Anything. But instead I just sat down and didn't say a word for the rest of the meet. Yes, I'm a sore loser, if that's what you wanna call it. To me, I just like to win. I only wanna win. Anything else is . . . false. Fake.

But real.

So real, I didn't even want to talk about it on the way to church the next day. Not with no one. Not even with God. I'd spent all morning braiding Maddy's hair the same way Ma used to braid mine when I was little. Only difference is Ma got fat fingers, and used to be braiding like she was trying to strip my edges or make me bald. Talkin' 'bout, "Gotta make it tight so it don't come loose." Right. But I don't even do Maddy's that tight, and I can knock out a whole head full of hair in half an hour if she sits still. Which she never does.

"How many more?" Maddy whined, squirming on the floor in front of me.

"I'm almost done. Just chill out, so I can . . ." I picked up the can of beads and shook them in her ear like one of them Spanish shaker things. And just like that, she calmed down and let me tilt her head forward so I could braid the last section, the bit of curls tightly wound at the base of her neck. I dipped my finger in the gunk on the back of my hand, then massaged it into Maddy's scalp. Then I stroked grease into the left-over bush-ball, tugging it straight, then letting it go, watching it shrink back into dark brown cotton candy.

"What colors you want?" I asked, separating the hair into the three parts.

"Ummmm . . ." Maddy put a finger to her chin, acting like she thinking. I say acting, because she knew what color she wanted. She picked the same one every week. Matter fact, there was only one color in the can.

"Red," we both said at the same time, me, of course, with a little more pepper and a little less pep. Maddy tried to whip around and give me a funny face, but I was mid-braid.

"Uh-uh. Stay still."

Then came the beading. Today, thirty braids. So, three red beads on each braid. Ninety beads. I used tiny bits of aluminum foil on the ends to keep the beads from slipping off, even though I knew they would anyway. But who got time to use those little rubber bands? Not me. And definitely not Maddy.

When we finished, Maddy did what she always did—ran to the bathroom. I followed her, like I always did, and lifted her up so she could see herself in the mirror. She smiled, her mouth like a piano with only one black key, one front tooth missing. Then Maddy ran back to the living room and blew a kiss at a picture propped up on the table next to the TV—the same picture every time—of me at her age, six, with a big cheese and a missing front tooth and braids, red beads, aluminum foil on the ends.

I do Maddy's hair every Sunday for two reasons. The first is because Momly can't do it. If it was up to her, Maddy's hair would be in two Afro-puffs every day. Either that, or Momly would've shaved it all off by now. It's not that she don't care. She does. It's just that she don't know what to do with hair like Maddy's— like ours. Ma do, but Momly . . . nope. She never had to deal with nothing like it, and there ain't no rule book for white people to know how to work with black hair. And her husband, my uncle Tony, he ain't no help. Ever since they adopted us, every time I talk about

Maddy's hair, Uncle Tony says the same thing—just let it rock. Like he's gonna sit in the back of Maddy's class and stink-face all the six-year-old bullies in barrettes. Right. But luckily for everybody, especially Maddy, I know what I'm doing. Been a black girl all my life.

The other reason I always do Maddy's hair on Sundays is because that's when we see Ma, and she don't wanna see Maddy looking like "she ain't never been nowhere." So after Maddy's hair is done, we get dressed. As in, dressed up. All the way up. Maddy puts on one of her church dresses, white patent leather shoes that most people only wear on Easter Sunday, but for us—for Ma—every Sunday is like Easter Sunday. I put on a dress too, run a comb through my hair until it cooperates. Ugly black ballerina flats because Ma don't want me "looking fast in the house of the Lord." Then Momly drives us across town to Barnaby Terrace, my old neighborhood.

Barnaby Terrace is . . . fine. I don't really know what else to say about it except for the fact that there's nothing really to say about it. Ain't nobody rich, that's for sure. But ain't nobody really poor, neither. Everybody's just regular. Regular people going to regular jobs having regular kids who go to regular schools and grow up to be regular people with regular jobs, and on and on. And I guess everything was pretty regular about me, too, until six years ago. Follow me. I'd just turned six, and me and my dad were having one of our famous invisible cupcake parties. Kinda like how little girls on old TV shows be having tea parties, but you know how it don't ever really be tea in the cups? Like that. Except I didn't have a tea set, and my mom wouldn't let us use her real teacups, which were really just random coffee mugs, plus my dad always said tea don't even taste good enough to pretend to drink it. He also said "tea" and "eat" are made of the same letters anyway, so pretending to eat was pretty much the same as pretending to drink. And what better thing to pretend to eat than cupcakes. And that's what we always had—imaginary cupcakes.

But on this night, my mother cut the party short because it was a school night, plus she was pregnant with Maddy at the time and needed my father to massage her feet. So he whispered in my ear, "Sleep tight, sweet Pancake, your mama and the Waffle need me." Then he kissed me good night—first on the forehead, then on one cheek, then on the other cheek. I don't know what happened next. My guess is that after rubbing Ma's feet, he kissed her good night too. And Maddy, the "Waffle" who was probably being all fidgety in Ma's stomach. I bet Dad smooched right on the belly button, then rolled over and went to sleep.

But he never woke up.

Like . . . ever.

It was crazy. And if we had been allowed to drink pretend tea from my mother's real cups, they all would've been shattered the next morning after she woke me up, her face wet with tears, and blurted, "Something's happened." I would've smashed each and every one of them cups on the floor. And I would've smashed more of them two years later when my mother had two toes cut off her right foot. And six months after that, when she had that whole foot cut off. And six months after that—three years ago—when my mother had both her legs chopped off, which, I'm telling you, would've left the whole stupid cabinet empty. Broken mugs everywhere. Nothing left to drink from.

But I didn't. Instead I just swallowed it all. And wished this was all some kind of invisible, pretend . . . something. But it wasn't.

And just so you don't get the wrong idea, it's not like my mom just wanted her legs cut off. She got the sugar. Well, it's really a disease called diabetes, but she calls it the sugar, so I call it the sugar, plus I like that better than diabetes because diabetes got the word "die" in it, and I hate that word. The sugar broke Ma's lower extremities, which is how doctors say legs. It just went crazy all in her body. Stopped the blood flow to her feet. I used to have to rub and grease them at night, just like my dad used to, and it was like putting lotion on two tree trunks. Dry and cracked. Swollen and dark like she'd been standing in coal. But at some point she just couldn't feel them no more, and I went from moisturizing them to trying to rub them back to life. And after that, they were basically . . . I guess the best way to explain it is to just say . . . dead. Her feet had died. Like I said, I hate that word, but ain't no way else to say it. And I guess death can travel, can spread like a fire in the body, so the doctors had to go ahead and cut her legs off—they call it "amputate," which for some reason makes me think of something growing, not something being chopped—just above the knee to keep more of her from dying.

Maddy's only six now, and ever since she was born I'd been helping out the best I could with her. But with Ma losing her toes and feet, helping out became straight-up taking care of. I'm talking about keeping lists in my head of things I had to take care of.

TO DO: Make sure Maddy's bathed.
TO DO: Make sure Maddy's dressed.

TO DO: Make sure Maddy's fed.
TO DO: Everything.

But after Ma lost her legs, my godparents—my dad's brother, Tony, and his wife, Emily—stepped in and took over as our "sole guardians," which, the first time I heard it, I thought was "soul guardians," which, I guess, is just as good. Kinda like guardian angels. I bet Uncle Tony and Auntie Emily—who Maddy used to call Mama Emily, which became Momly—had no idea that when they said they would be our godparents they were inheriting all this drama. I bet they just thought they'd have to give us gifts on random days—days that wasn't our birthday or Christmas. Slip us ten-dollar bills just because. Stuff like that. Not take care of us, all the way. That's . . . a lot. But they always acted like they were cool with it—like this is what they signed up for—and we grateful, even though I still gotta look out for Maddy because, you know . . . I just do. I still keep a list in my brain. Plus, Momly can't do black hair for nothing.

Why am I telling you this long story?

Oh, I remember.

Because, Sundays. On Sundays, like I said, Maddy's hair gotta be right. For Ma.

TO DO: Dance like my mother's watching
(or like I'm killing roaches)

ONCE WE GET to Ma's house—our old . . . other house—it goes the same way every time. Maddy jumps out and runs to the door, her red beads clacking with every step, the foil on the ends glinting like each braid was a Fourth of July sparkler. I jump out behind her.

"Only ring it once," I tell her, just because ringing anybody's doorbell ten million times is one of Maddy's favorite things to do. But with Ma, a person who can't walk, it comes across as a hurry up, which is rude.

"I know, I know," Maddy says, acting like she wasn't about to go hammer-time on the doorbell.

"Coming!" Ma's muffled voice comes through the wooden door. By the time she opens it, Momly has parked the car and is standing with us, still rubbing sleep off her face, dressed in scrubs and those weird Wiffle-ball shoes that look too uncomfortable to walk in. But that's Momly.

"Praise the Lord," Ma sings, wheeling the chair back to give us enough space to come inside. Maddy gives the first big hug. She always does, and Ma receives it as if she'd just caught a wedding bouquet.

"Maddy, my Waffle." Big smile. "Girl, you get bigger every time I see you. And prettier."

"But you just saw me last week."

"Yep, and you bigger and prettier," Ma says, beaming. It's the same thing every week. You would think they'd switch it up, but they don't. It's a routine we all need, I guess. Something to remind us that even though life with Momly and Uncle Tony is good, Ma is who we are. Where we from. Blood.

Once Maddy gets done gushing, I bend down and give Ma a kiss on the cheek. Her skin is dry, rough on my lips, and I know better than to put any gloss on because that's also "too fast for church." She smells like flowers dipped in cake batter. And hair grease. Familiar.

"Hi, baby," she says, taking my hand.

"Hi, Ma." I squeeze. She squeezes back.

I wheel Ma—always wearing a colorful, patterned dress, her hair in fresh straw curls—out to the passenger side of the car. She can do it by herself, but I like to do it for her. Just used to it, I guess. Sometimes Momly tries to help, but she knows this is my thing. Take care of Maddy, then take care of Ma. I open the car door, put the brakes on the chair so it don't roll out from under my mother as she hoists herself up and leans into the car. Then she whips what's left of her legs in. After that, I check to make sure none of her dress is hanging out. Then I close the door and roll the wheelchair to the back of the car, where I fold it up and put it in the trunk. There's an art to this, because if I do it wrong, and the wheels of the chair bump up against me, it'll dirty up my dress, and then I'll have to hear Ma's mouth the whole way to church and back about how "cleanliness is next to godliness." But I always do it right, because ain't nobody got time for no lectures.

Next comes the pre-church small talk.

"So, how was the week?" Ma, who always immediately turns off the car radio (Momly only listens to talk talk talk anyway), asks Momly as we back out of the driveway. This, of course, is a real false start, a fake beginning to a conversation, only because Ma and

Momly speak like six thousand times a week. But this was Ma's way of opening up a discussion in a behind-the-back kind of way, to say whatever she wanted to say to me and Maddy. That way, it don't seem like Momly's a snitch. Even though I know Momly be snitching. I mean, she's our aunt. And our adopted mother. Blabbing just comes with the territory.

"Nothing crazy to report. Maddy brought home all fours in school." That was Momly's lead-in this week.

"Fours, huh? Is that like an A?" Ma asked this all the time, and I couldn't tell if she really had a hard time keeping up with the grading system of our charter school or if she was just being shady. She always called the grading system new wave, and said things like, *Charter don't mean smarter*.

Ma cracked the window to let some air in. Momly's car always smelled like a freshly scrubbed bathtub. Like . . . clean, but poisonous. Cleanliness was next to godliness, huh? So next to godliness that you might die from it. Maddy and me were used to it, but it irritated Ma every single time she was in the car.

"Yes, Ma. That's an A, remember?" Maddy piped up from the backseat. Ma didn't turn around. Just nodded.

"And Patty, well, she's really doing great on the new track team. Patty, did you bring the ribbon?" I caught

Momly's eye in the rearview mirror. She knew I ain't bring no ribbon. What I look like bringing a ribbon to church? I knew what she was doing. But if there was one thing I didn't want to talk about this Sunday, it was running. Like I said, I'm a sore loser. And petty, too. And now, instantly annoyed.

"I forgot," I said, flat.

"Well, let me tell you, Bev, she came in second in—"

"But what about grades? Is she gettin' fours or fives or whatever?" My mother cut Momly off mid-brag. Ugh. If there was a second thing I didn't want to talk about this Sunday, it was school.

"We're getting there. She's still getting used to it. Still adjusting."

The "it" they were talking about was my new school. Up until this year, I was at Barnaby Elementary, then Barnaby Middle, which are both public schools in my old neighborhood. Ma thought it would be best if I "transitioned smoothly" out of living with her by keeping me at my regular school where all my friends go. Brianna, Deena, and especially my day-one, Ashley, who everybody calls Cotton. Me and Cotton been friends since kindergarten, back when Lu Richardson's mother was our babysitter and she used to help us make up dance routines to nineties R & B. Dance routines we still know but I don't do no more. But Cotton still does. And without me at school with her, who was gonna tape her bathroom dance-offs? Better yet, who was gonna blame her stinky farts on the boys? Who was gonna tell her that her hair is gonna be cute as soon as the curls fall? Maybe Brianna and Deena would, but that wasn't their job. It was mine. But I couldn't do it like I needed to because now I was in a different part of the city, somewhat settled into life with Uncle Tony and Momly, and going to this corny new school *they* picked—because it was a much shorter drive—over in Sunny Lancaster's neighborhood (he's another newbie on the track team). Which means, from Barnaby Terrace to Bougie Terrace. Well, the school was really called Chester Academy, which was a dead giveaway it was bougie. I mean, the cornballs who named the place thought it was too good to even be called a school. An academy? Whatever. Anyway, being at Chester was . . . different. Like, real different. First of all, we had to wear uniforms. Pleated skirts and stiff button-ups. And it was all girls, and let's just say, not too many of them had real nicknames. Not too many of them had mothers that smelled like hair grease. Hair gel? Yes. But hair grease? Nah.

"Well, I suggest she get used to it soon, or there won't

be no more running," Ma said. Momly caught my eyes again in the mirror. Winked. She knew Ma was hard on me about school, but she also knew I had to run.

As Momly pulled up in front of the church, she said what she always said every week. "Y'all say a prayer for me and your uncle."

And my mother said what she always said in response: "Lord knows y'all need it."

Momly and Uncle Tony never went to church, but when my mother made the arrangements for me and Maddy to live with them, it was under the condition that we wouldn't miss a service. A whole lot of talk about grace and faith and mercy and salvation, which, to me, all just equaled shouting, clapping, and singing in a building built to be a sweatbox. A constant reminder that all that hair combing I did before coming was a waste of time, as it was a guarantee that I'd be leaving with my curls shriveled up into a frizzy lopsided cloud.

Because of my mother's wheelchair, she had to sit in the aisle, while me and Maddy sat in a pew. And throughout the whole beginning of the service, Ma would peer down the pew to make sure we were behaving, which was hard because we always sat in the row with the stinky Thomases. Mr. and Mrs. Thomas been smelling like they just puked up mothballs for as long as I've known them. They always took the back pew, which is where we sat, so, yeah, most of the time I was sitting real still praying to God not to let me suffocate. *Lord, please bless them with some soap. Some perfume. Anything. Make a miracle happen*, or, *What have I done to deserve this? Father, why hath thou forsaken me?*

But there's one part of the service where Ma always eases up on acting like a warden. And that's when Pastor Carter starts sweating, and Sister Jefferson starts laughing. See, when the sweat and laughter comes, that basically means the spirit is in the building. And when Pastor starts banging his hand on the pulpit, and throws out one of those everybody-knows-it scriptures like, "Yea, though I walk through the valley of the shadow of death," that's the cue for the organ player, Dante, to get ready to play the happy music. Happy music sounds like the music they play at the beginning of baseball games, except sped up, and looped over and over and over again, until every lady in the church catches the spirit. And when you catch the spirit, that don't mean you reach out and grab it like it's ball or something. It's not like that. Catching the spirit is more like the spirit catching you. And when it happens, you dance. But not like *dance* dance. Not like Cotton be dancing. You dance like the church is roach infested and it's your job to step on them all. Like you trying to put a hole in the floor. Like you trying to break the heel off your white church pumps.

And Ma loves this. She always has. But now, she can't dance. So, when she looks down the aisle during this part, it's because she wants to see me and Maddy catch the spirit. Actually, she just wants to see us do a triple-time step. See us move our legs a million miles a minute. Maddy loves it. As soon as she hears the music, she gets to bouncing around in her seat the same way she does when I'm doing her hair. Me, well, I don't ever really feel nothing. But I love my mother. So I give Maddy the look, and she stands up, shoulders rocking, silly smile smeared across her lips, but only for a second before she mimics the other "saints" and screws her face up like she just caught another whiff of the Thomases. Then I stand up. Ma rolls the wheelchair back so we have enough space to slide out of the pew without tripping or brushing against the wheels of her chair and dirtying up our holy dresses.

And once we're out, oh . . . it's party time. More like, workout time. It's like black Riverdance, or something like that. Actually, it reminds me of some of the warm-up drills Coach makes us do at practice. High knees. Footwork. And Ma loves it. But she can't fist-pump and yell, "Go, Maddy! Go, Patty! Go! Go! Go!"

in church. Not really appropriate. But what she can do is yell, "Yes, Lawd! Yessssss! Thank ya, Lawd! Thank ya!" And that's basically the same thing.

After service, Momly is always waiting for us, and I go through the same process—getting Ma in the car, the wheelchair in the trunk. The only difference is on the ride home, Ma's all high off Jesus and now ready to talk about what I'm normally doing great at, even though not so great this week. Running.

"You know I pray for you. I pray God put something special in your legs, in your muscles so you can run and not grow weary," she said, lifting a finger in the air, proud that she was able to slip a Bible verse into regular conversation, a thing she was always trying to do.

"She's really something, Bev," Momly adds. I hate when they try to make me feel better by talking around me, like I'm not right here.

I lost.

I lost, I lost, I lost.

I sit in the back, clenching my jaw. Maddy sits next to me, kicking the back of Momly's seat.

"Oh, I know she is, because she's mine." Ma turns around and this time beams at me. "And I don't make no junk."

TO DO: Introduce myself
(which I should've done a while ago)

I SHOULD PROBABLY introduce myself. My name is Patina Jones. And I ain't no junk. I also ain't no hair flipper. And most of the girls at Chester Academy are hair flippers who be looking at me like my mom some kind of junk maker. But ain't none of them got the guts to come out of their mouths with no craziness. They just turn and flip their dingy ponytails toward me like I care. Tuh. I guess it's no secret that it's never easy being the new girl. And I get to be the new girl in two different places—on the Defenders team, and at Chester. Lucky me. But at least the Defenders I can deal with because I know, for a fact, I can run.

I've been running track for three years now, thanks to Uncle Tony. Well, not just him. It really has more to do with my mom, dad, Uncle Tony, and Maddy. My whole family. But let's just say Uncle Tony okeydoked the idea into my brain. See, it was my dad's birthday, and also a few months before my mother's legs were taken, and we were celebrating with cupcakes—real cupcakes, not pretend ones—that my mother had baked in honor of him. Yellow cake, strawberry icing, Dad's recipe. It had become a tradition that I loved, even though it always made me sad. It was really just a chance for everybody to sit around and for the old-heads to crack jokes and tell me and Maddy stories about him. Maddy never knew him. And even though I did, and I remember him—I'll never, ever forget him—there were a lot of things I just didn't know. Like how he used to make beats, and sell instrumental tapes to aspiring rappers and singers in the neighborhood. And how he used the money he made from that to put himself through culinary school to become a pastry chef. And how he loved letting me lick the batter off the spoon before baking a cake, but not nearly as much as he loved seeing me chomp down on the finished product. But apparently, according to Uncle Tony, none of these things were as sweet to him as seeing me run.

"Your daddy called me when you took your first step," Uncle Tony, peeling the paper from his cupcake, explained in the middle of an I-remember-when session. "I answered the phone and Ronnie just started yelling, 'She did it, Toon! My baby did it!'" Toon was what my dad called Uncle Tony, a nickname from when they were kids back when Uncle Tony was obsessed with, you guessed it, cartoons.

"He sure did. He was so proud his Pancake was walking," Ma confirmed, smirking like this memory didn't bother her, even though the shine in her eyes said different. Maddy, who was too young to really care about any of this, listened in, cupcake icing smeared all over her chin. Didn't really make sense for me to wipe her mouth until she was done making a mess. The things you learn.

"But when you started running . . ." Uncle Tony shook his head. "That's when he really lost it. He'd send me videos every other day of you dashing back and forth across the room. Little fat legs just movin'! But you'd have thought you'd grown wings and started flying or something the way Ronnie was acting." Uncle Tony licked pink frosting off the cupcake and went on. "I don't know what it was about seeing you move like that. But your daddy loved it. You were definitely his Pancake, but you were also his little sprinter."

Before then, I never even thought about running. It didn't even cross my mind, even though I used to smoke all the boys in gym class at school, including Lu, who would get all in his feelings and be almost about to cry. Lu would be so salty, frontin' like he wasn't impressed, which didn't matter because running ain't mean nothing to me anyway. Not like . . . for real. But after hearing Uncle Tony talk about my dad like that, something clicked. And one night, a few months later, after Ma's legs were gone, after a crazy moment with Maddy—and I do mean crazy—that I'll also get to later on, I asked Momly and Uncle Tony to sign me up on a team. And they jumped to it because to them, it was also a good way for me to, I guess, deal with all the changes I was going through. Balance out all the unregul . . . um, wild stuff.

So proving myself on this new track team—the Defenders—was still just . . . running. Even if it was "elite." I mean, no matter how you look at it, it's still, listen to your coaches at practice, and wait to hear the gun at the meets. Then . . . run. Nothing to it. But proving myself at Chester Academy (also "elite") was trickier—way trickier—because there were no practices, no coaches, and no starter pistols telling me when to leave everybody in the dust. Matter fact, ain't even no dust at Chester, and running ain't nothing these girls are concerned with at all. Unless it was running their mouths.

Chester Academy is one of those schools that go from kindergarten all the way up to twelfth grade, but the different levels are broken into three wings of the building. The south wing, which was where the high school was. The east wing, which was sixth, seventh, and eighth grade. And the north wing, which was elementary, Maddy's domain. Yep, she's at Chester too, and she loves it, but that's because this the only school she's ever been at. She's never been in a school where you didn't have to wear pleated paper bags. She never went to a school with boys, and yes, boys make school really, really annoying sometimes, but they also can make it pretty fun. Or at least funny. Maddy never went to a school with mostly black kids either. She's only known life as a "raisin in milk," as my Ma puts it, where lunch is sautéed prawn, which ain't nothing but a fancy way to say cooked shrimp, and this stuff called couscous, which is basically just grits without the glob. Me, I'm a proud product of the Barnaby Terrace school system, where we ate nasty rectangle pizza (I don't miss that part) and drank chocolate milk for lunch. Where we played pranks on people and traded candy while talking trash after school. Where we had . . . fun.

Chester . . . well, I ain't had one second of fun at Chester yet. Matter fact, when I walk down that busy hall in the morning, I keep my eyes down. Focus on the floor because I ain't got time to get stunted on by a whole bunch of rich girls whose daddies own stuff. Not like cars and clothes, though they got those, too. But stuff like . . . boats. Ain't even no water nowhere near here, but these fools got BOATS! And they don't just own their houses, they own buildings! And businesses! Not like a corner store or a weekend dinner-plate situation or nothing like that. I'm talking biz-niss-sizz. My dad . . . he wanted to start his own business, another one of those birthday stories. A cupcake shop. And maybe if he didn't . . . never wake up . . . he would've done it. But I bet he wouldn't have bought no boat. But that's who these girls' daddies were. What they did. And if your daddy got himself a boat, and a building, what does he get you? Probably some kinda crazy pet, like a horse. (Can you even teach a horse how to guard your house?)

The other thing about these girls is that it seems like they ain't never been told they can't do nothing.

Never. I mean, they be wearing full faces of makeup and everything. Do you know what my mother would do if she saw me with my whole face made up for school like I was about to go on some kinda fashion photo shoot or something? She'd probably try to run over me with that wheelchair. But here, at Chester, as long as your face is selfie-ready 100 percent of the time, you got a chance. A chance at what? Well, I don't really know. All I know is, I ain't got one.

What I got is track. I got Ghost, Sunny, and I can't believe I'm gonna say this . . . Lu. That's what I got. Who I got. So I don't really care about the selfie-readies.

Well, that's not totally true. I care a little bit.

"So . . . what y'all do this weekend?" I asked Taylor Stein, Teylor Dorsey, and Becca Broward. It was Monday, in history class, which meant it was also the second day of the worst group project of all time in the history of life. The four of us had been lumped together last Friday to start on this assignment about an important woman from the past, and in two weeks we would have to do a presentation on her. On Friday all we did was nail down who we were going to focus on. My first choice was my hero, Florence "Flo Jo" Joyner, but none of the girls in my group knew who she was. Seriously? How do you not know one of the flyest runners to ever take a lap? There was a woman named Madeline Manning, who was probably the best American eight-hundred-meter runner, and that's my race, but still, Flo Jo was it. Plus, those nails . . . She looked like she raced during the day and was in a singing group at night.

So, anyway, then I tossed out my second choice, which was Harriet Tubman, who to me, was also a pretty good suggestion. Running from slavery and then coming back all those times to free everybody else—like a relay through the Underground Railroad— and Uncle Tony said she might be the new face of the twenty-dollar bill. That's major. But the girls weren't feeling that, either. And these are the moments I miss not going to school with Cotton, because she would've been like, "Yo, you know how crazy it would be to see my face on money? Like a hundred-dollar bill? I'd be framed in every corner store in the hood—your girl, lookin' like money, on money!" But that's not how the conversation went in my history group. Instead it was all, Harriet Tubman's just too serious. So when I asked who they were thinking about, Becca, who was one of these girls who swore she was gonna be a star when she grew up, said we should do the project on this lady named Sally Ride.

"First woman in space," she said, strangely pointing up at the ceiling. Okay. I can't front. Not a bad suggestion. But then Taylor said, for the second time, all these choices were too serious, as if the topic wasn't a serious topic. I mean, it's hard to be seen as important if you ain't never been through nothing serious. But Teylor, who goes by TeeTee (one of the few nicknames) decided to add her two cents (by the way, I'd want my face on the penny, because pennies be everywhere and they'd get my skin tone right) and muddy up our brainstorming session with the . . . uh . . . brilliant suggestion of Taylor Swift. Becca didn't say nothing. And I wanted to shoot it down, because we already had a Taylor and a Teylor in the group and I just couldn't take another one. But thankfully, Taylor hit TeeTee with a swift no.

So since serious was all I kept hearing on Friday, I decided to keep Monday light by trying out some of that "Momly-Ma special." Some good ol' small talk. And no, I don't know why I care, why these girls in my class matter to me, except for the fact that I'm just trying to make the best of the situation. I figured weekends had to be a common bond. I mean, it don't matter who you are, Saturday is Saturday.

"This weekend, well . . . ," TeeTee started. She used

the long, skinny part of a pen cap to scrape grime from under her nails. "Saturday, I hit the mall."

"Me too," Taylor followed.

"I know you did, because you were with me!" TeeTee squealed to Taylor, clenching her fingers into a bear paw to check her nails. Oh, I guess I should make clear that TeeTee and Taylor are best friends. Besties. Another word I don't like. It's just stupid. Bestie and best friend take the exact same amount of time to say. It ain't like an abbreviation. That's like me calling my teammates my teamies. Anyway, not only are Taylor and TeeTee best friends, but they're also cousins (cuzzies) and pretend to be sisters (sissies). They're like attached at the ponytail and call themselves T-N-T, which is funny because most of the time I just wished they'd explode.

Here's my issues, not with bestie-cousin-sisters, but with group projects: (1) One of the group members always has to volunteer their house for everyone to go over to and work on the presentation, which was never really a good thing because (2a) ain't nobody coming to my house and I don't wanna go to theirs, and (2b) only one person in the group actually does any work, which brings me to (3) that person is me. So as the T(a/e)ylors started going on about whether or not they should both take a T-shirt—the same exact T-shirt—back to exchange it for a smaller size, and Becca was off in space, it was me who reached into my backpack and pulled out printouts of images of this Mexican painter lady, Frida Kahlo. I'd swiped them from the Internet over the weekend. Frida Kahlo was who we all settled on on Friday, by the way, with the help of Ms. Lanford, who figured political stuff, sick stuff, service stuff, and art stuff could all be explored in the life of this one artist. I was cool with it. I mean, she wasn't Harriet or Flo Jo, but this lady, Frida, wore suits, stood up to dudes, and had issues with her legs. Good enough for me.

After a few seconds of the other girls looking at the images, I got tired of waiting for them to ask how my weekend was. Not like they would've cared about me cooking Maddy's breakfast, making sure she ate her dinner, doing Maddy's hair, church with the Ma (and the stinky Thomases), then letting Maddy crawl in bed with me last night while I counted all the beads in her hair, one by one, hoping she'd be asleep before I got to ninety, plus on top of all that, finding time to research Frida Kahlo for this project and not go to the mall. Oh, and I had to run. But still, I was waiting for them to ask. Waiting for them to be normal. Or at least treat me normal.

"Well, I had a track meet," I threw out there, out of the blue, not like I really wanted to talk about that, either, but I was willing to just try to connect or whatever.

"Whoa. This lady is in desperate need of some tweezers," Taylor said, actually pinching the paper between Frida Kahlo's eyes.

"Came in first in the eight hundred meter," I lied, still waiting on someone, anyone to say something about it. To acknowledge me. But before anyone did, Ms. Lanford popped over to check on us.

"How are we doing, ladies?" Ms. Lanford was now standing beside our desks, which had been pushed together into a square, all of us facing each other, the pictures of Frida—bright-colored self-portraits including monkeys, birds, and flowers—spread out.

The girls all flashed toothpaste-commercial smiles and gave different versions of "Good." I bit my bottom lip and prayed for the bell.

After school I never waste time at my locker. I scurry down to the end of the main corridor, eyes darting from forward to floor, through the mess of hair flippers, the wrath-letes (kids who feel like it's a sport to make everyone's life miserable), the know-it-alls, the knownothins, the hush-hushes (super quiet, super shy), the YMBCs (You Might be Cuckoo)—the girls who wear all black and cover their backpacks with buttons and pins—and the girls whose boyfriends, brothers, and fathers all wear khaki pants. Every. Day. I know this sounds kinda mean, but it's real. So real. It's like a rich kid obstacle course, and once I make it all the way to the end, I walk through the courtyard to the north wing, where I then have to maneuver through the younger version of all those same categories. Except way cuter. And less annoying. And the cutest and least annoying of them all (in my opinion) is Maddy, who I always find waiting for me just outside her teacher Mrs. Stein's, who she calls Mrs. S's, door.

"Ready?" I ask, awkwardly wrapping my arms around her detachable hunchback she calls a backpack, only way I can get a hug in with that thing on.

"Yep." She turns around and throws the peace sign up to her friends, then turns back and squeezes me, tries to lift me. It's something she's been doing for a while. She has a weird obsession with being strong, with proving she can lift heavy things. She got it (and the peace sign thing too) from Uncle Tony, who used to do push-ups with Maddy sitting on his back, counting in a cartoon voice. Mickey Mouse. Goofy. *Goofy*.

Anyway, after Maddy's cheese and squeeze, we head out to meet Momly, who is always there on time to meet us in the car pickup line.

I'm sure I don't have to tell you what the ride home was like. Maddy . . . talking.

Mona got glue in her hair. Again.

I picked Willa up.

Lauren cried six times.

You know Willa, right? She bigger than me.

Mrs. S's birthday is on Thursday. I think she's turning like eighty.

She's so lucky she gets to spend it at the farm.

We'll try to get the cows to moo "Happy Birthday" to her.

Oh, don't forget you have to drive me to the farm on Thursday, Momly.

Mrs. S reminded us. So I'm reminding you.

Hopefully Lauren won't cry the whole time.

Anyway, Riley wouldn't pass the ball to me at first. But then she did. And then I passed it back. And then she passed it to Rachel. And then . . .

While Maddy . . . Maddied . . . I changed my clothes in the backseat. It was my daily shape-shifting routine, which wasn't a big deal because I always wore my shorts under my skirt, and a tank top under my button-up, so that by the time we reached MLK Park—my homework started—and I told Maddy what I told her every day, that I'd help her with hers after practice, I was ready to jump out and run from my motormouthed little sister and hit the track. Which, I gotta admit for me, even with just a second-place ribbon, was sometimes more home than home.

TO DO: Get over it
(I mean, the whole second place thing)

"STRAIGHTEN UP, PATTY!" Momly called out from the car window before pulling off. She said this all the time. Drove me crazy. Always nagging me about my posture or whatever. *Roll your shoulders back, Patty. Stop hunching, Patty.* And even though it was annoying, I knew she was right. I always walked like I had on a backpack, even when I didn't. *You'll be walking with a cane by the time you're my age, Patty.* And even though Momly's age was a long, long, lonnnng way away, I wasn't trying to be walking with no cane by then. Or ever. So, I shook off the nag and rolled my shoulders back.

I made it all the way to the track with my back straight and caught up with Ghost and Lu going on about some dude who Ghost, I guessed, was having beef with at school.

"Soon as spring break is over, we'll see if he got something to say to me," Ghost said.

"Man, he ain't gon' say nothin'. He ain't even gon' look your way. Probably at home right now still crying about getting smoked on Saturday," Lu followed.

"Burnt him up. Might've ruined his little vacation," Ghost topped off, laughing and slapping Lu's hand. Those two were always braggin' about something. That was regular. So regular that I let my shoulders roll forward again, comfortable. Just couldn't help it. Plus, these fools, and just about everybody else on our team, were already on break, and I was still in school getting academied. Fancy School Patty. And I didn't know if Sunny was on break or not because he gets home-schooled, which, to me, just seemed like vacation with a little bit of education sprinkled in. Sunny didn't seem to be paying Ghost and Lu no mind, though. He was just sitting on the track with his feet pressed together, his long legs butterflied.

"Wassup, Patty?" Lu said.

"Wassup," I said with nothing on it. I sat next to

Sunny, stretched my legs out in front of me. I was trying to get my mind right. Trying to refocus, work harder. First practice of a new week—after the first meet. Time to get to work. Ghost just looked at me and nodded. Probably could see the serious on my face, so he knew not to say nothing. Too bad Aaron, our team captain, didn't get it.

"Yo, Patty, you still mad?" Aaron asked, stoking a fire he pretended he didn't know was there. I didn't think he was necessarily trying to be mean, but . . . he knew it was a soft spot, especially since the reason he was asking was because of the way I had acted when I crossed the finish line.

Now, Ghost was giving Aaron a *what's your problem* look. "Yo, chill!" he warned. But the truth is, I didn't need Ghost or Lu or Sunny or anybody to take up for me. But I didn't say nothing. Just let it ride.

"I'm just sayin', it was the first race of the season," Aaron bulldozed on. "Let it go. Ain't no reason to be mad about losing." Losing? Losing? Back went my shoulders, and out came the mad.

"Yeah, maybe for you," I shot back, glaring at Aaron. "But I'm still mad. And so what?"

"Uh-oh," Curron warned. He was a mid-distance runner like me, but had more mouth than he had moves, so he already knew the power of my clapback.

"Shut up, Curron," Aaron spat. "Yo, Patty, I ain't even mean it like that. It's just you got second place and was acting all funky for the rest of the meet, like no one else had races to run, like you ain't got team-mates that needed your support." Spoken like a true captain.

I didn't respond. Just stretched my arms out in front of me and grabbed my left foot, pulled myself down until my head was on my knee. Sunny was doing the same stretch. I turned my face so that my cheek was resting on my kneecap, and caught his eyes catching my legs.

"Hey, Patty," he said, in his usual sweet voice, which in this moment seemed a little creepy. Actually, a lot creepy. He looked down my leg awkwardly and flashed a timid smile.

"Hey . . . uh, Sunny," I replied, uncomfortable. Was Sunny checkin' me out? If he was, now was not the time. Also . . . no . . . gross . . . stop it . . . right now . . . seriously.

"What happened to your nails?" he asked. Oh, he was checkin' out my nails, and the fact that there was no polish on them. But there had been on Saturday at the meet. I did my best to make a cool design using the Defenders' colors, but it ended up just looking like bright blue with orange squiggles. I scrubbed them clean before church yesterday—another thing Ma would've said made me look too fast. Ugh, yeah . . . I know. That's the point. But Ma was talking about a different kind of fast.

"I took the polish off," I said. "Why?"

"Oh, just because they were cool. Reminded me of Flo Jo," Sunny said with a shrug. I wanted to ask him how he even knew about Flo Jo's nails, but I didn't. Because there was no need. Because he obviously knew something. I did, however, let a smile inch onto my face for the first time since the race. The first time in two days.

"Okay, listen up," Coach said. He'd been standing off to the side talking to Whit, the assistant coach. But now he was in front of us, clapping his hands together to get our attention. "Before we start practice, I first want to say good job on Saturday. Some of you did better than others, but all of you put your hearts into it. I saw some things on the track that I loved"—then he looked straight at me—"and I saw some things that didn't quite rub me right. Either way, I'm proud." He pulled something from his back pocket. A metal stick. A baton. "But now, we got work to do." He told everyone else to go start their warm-up laps, but he asked me to stay behind. And once everyone else had a two-hundred-meter head start, Coach "invited" me to jog with him. That's right, Coach was running. And he never ran. He just ordered us to run. Even though we all knew about his whole used-to-be-an-Olympian thing, it was so hard to believe because we never saw him even pretend to take a stride.

After about ten seconds of nothing but the sound of rubber on asphalt, Coach finally said, "You did good Saturday, kid," the silver of the baton gleaming in the sun.

Jog, jog, jog.

I let my arms drop down to my side, shook them out. "I did okay," I said, blah.

"Second place is a lot more than okay," Coach replied, clearly trying to make me feel better. "Still got you a piece of fabric, didn't it?"

The piece of fabric Coach was talking about was the ribbon. The second-place ribbon. The not-first-place second-place ribbon. The one they give you for false finishes. "Yeah, I guess."

Jog, jog, jog, jog.

"Here." He extended the baton to me. I took it, not sure why he was giving it to me, but it didn't matter

45

because as soon as I took it, he said, "Now give it back." I gave it back and about two seconds later, he extended it toward me again. "Take it." Confused and getting annoyed, I grabbed it again. "Give it to me," he said, motioning for it almost immediately, his palm up, rising and falling with each step. We were almost a whole lap around, and I could see my teammates well into their second and final one. I slapped the baton into Coach's hand again and this time asked, "What we doin' this for?"

"Take it," he said, passing it to me a third time.

Jog, jog, jog.

"Coach, why you doin' this?" I repeated. My attitude started to sizzle as I reluctantly took the baton again.

"I'll tell you. But first"—jog, jog, jog—"give it back to me."

I ticked my tongue against my teeth and gave Coach the bar, the metal clinking against his wedding ring. Finally he was ready to stop being a weirdo and tell me whatever it was he was trying to get me to understand.

"How did it feel in your hand?"

Jog, jog, jog, jog.

"I don't know," I said, trying to find an answer. "I guess . . . normal?"

"Right. It felt normal, every time it went from my hand to yours, and from yours to mine." Coach passed the baton from one hand to the next. "Now imagine it's got magic powers, and every time I give it to you I'm transferring some kind of power from me to you. Like strength, or something. And when you pass it back, you transfer your power to me. So we stay balanced. Now if for some reason you decide not to pass it to me, what do you think happens?

"I don't get your strength," I said in the voice I give the hair flippers when they tell me I should try "a little powder on my nose." The *whatever* voice.

"Exactly." Jog, jog. Coach cleared his throat and tried to sound as if he wasn't winded, but I knew he was because his words were thinning out. "Now this baton represents the energy of our team. When we're passing it from one person to the next, the team's energy stays, like you said, normal. But if anyone decides they don't want to pass it, they don't want to participate in it, well then, that energy is knocked off balance and your teammates are left empty-handed. Weakened. You understand?"

So here's what I was figuring about Coach. He was probably one of those kids who wrote poetry and stuff like that. He acts all cool, but the way he be talking makes me think he was more like Sunny when he was younger. Which is still cool. But a different kind of cool. And I don't really know if all his philosophies make sense, but we all understand what he be trying to tell us, no matter how left he gotta take us to get us right.

So, "I think so," is what I said back to him.

Coach cut his eyes at me—not satisfied.

"Well, to make sure you know so, let me make it clear. We are a team, Patty. You can pout and shout, but you can*not* check out." Coach took a second before praising himself. "I should've been a rapper. Out here running on a track when I should've been rapping on a track!" He laughed. I did too, an inside belly chuckle. "So, you understand now?"

"Yeah."

"Good, because I don't feel like running no more." Coach made a hard left off the track and started walking across the grass. He flipped the baton in his hand over and over. "Hurry up and finish, Patina. . . ." Patina. Coach was always trying to be funny, and I knew he thought saying my name like that was comedy gold. He lifted the baton in the air like a wizard casting a spell and yelled, "We got work to do!"

TO DO: Dance, this time, like an old king is watching (stiff and boring)

BY THE TIME I reached the other side of the track, Coach was already laying out what everyone needed to do in practice, which, for the most part, was basically what we always did on Mondays. Fartleks—fart licks—which is basically just when you run kinda fast for three minutes then real fast for one minute. Then kinda fast for three, real fast for one. Over and over and over again. Then there's some specialized training, where the sprinters would break off and do their own thing, the mid-distance runners would do the same, and the distance runners, well . . . they just run all practice. But then, out of nowhere, Coach threw a wrench in the plan.

"We're also gonna spend some time working on relay," he said, slapping the baton against his thigh. "Not all twenty of you."

"There's nineteen of us, Coach. Chris is gone, remember?" Aaron slipped in. Coach just raised his eyebrows, glared at Aaron in the *I'm talkin'* way. Plus, rounding up ain't against the rules. Seriously.

"Anyway, just my mid-distance runners for now," Coach elaborated. "At some point we'll develop the 4x400, but we don't have enough veteran sprinters on the boys' side for that. He nodded at Ghost and Lu. "We'll get you newbies where you need to be soon. We got a long season ahead of us. But for now, let's start with one of our sweet spots—the 4x800. Let me get Freddy, Mikey, Eric, and Curron. And for the girls, I need Deja, Krystal, Brit-Brat, and joining them as the fourth will be Patty." He glared at me. "Can you handle that?" I nodded. "Good. Coach Whit is gonna work with y'all. These two groups are our 4x800 relay teams. If anyone has a problem with this decision, speak now or forever hold your peace."

I looked around the circle at all the faces, each one either nodding or smirking. I was cool with running relay, even though I never had before. I've watched it enough times—at meets, the Olympic races they show on TV, and Internet clips—to know that all you had to do was take the baton, then run as fast as you could to hand it off to the next person. Like passing the collection plate at church.

"All right, ladies, come this way," Coach Whit called, leading me and the other three girls to the outside of the track. She was holding a small radio, one of the old ones with a CD player and a handle. The kind Cotton's grandma got in her kitchen. Whit set it on the track. Then she gave us what I can only describe as an evil grin. "Today, I'm gonna teach y'all how to dance."

Wait. What?

"Dance?" Brit-Brat bawked. "I don't know about them"—she thumbed at us—"but I already know how to do that." She put her hands together in a single clap, then put them up to her chest, palms out, and started shoving the air—a standing push-up—like they did on the old-school rap videos my father made me watch. Salt-N-Pepa style.

"Heyyyyy!" Deja howled, joining in, dipping low.

"Go, Deja! Go, Brit-Brat! Go, Deja! Go, Brit-Brat! It's your birthday, but not really. We at track practice.

We at track practice. Track, track, track, track!" Krystal chanted.

I didn't join them, but their silly dancing definitely helped with the process of pulling me out of my second-place slump. Brit-Brat's craziness reminded me so much of Cotton's, jumping around, clapping, telling me to make sure I'm getting good angles with the phone. This was something Taylor and TeeTee and Becca, and all the hair flippers I went to school with, couldn't do. What I was missing. Even so, though me and the girls on the track team could kinda relate, I was still the new girl, and I hadn't really gotten close to everybody yet. At least, not the vets. My crew were the newbies, and the only one of them I could see breaking out in a full-on dance break was Sunny—which would be the funniest dance break of all time, with his lanky self. So I didn't feel like I could really join in. But Brit-Brat's goofiness definitely made me feel like maybe I could vibe with them. Maybe next time. Like maybe the vets were cool.

"Okay, okay." Coach Whit tried to settle us down and hold in her laugh at the same time. "You do know there are other dances that don't involve all that booty action, right?"

"Whatever, Whit. You probably be just like this in

the club," Brit-Brat said, tapping Deja with the back of her hand.

"You be goin' to the club, Whit?" Deja asked, smiling all silly.

"None of your business. And this is not the club," Whit shut them down, shaking her head. "Anyway, we're gonna learn a different kind of dancing." She pushed play on the radio. And the music that came out wasn't . . . it wasn't classical, but . . .

"Oh, so the track ain't good enough to be a club, but it is good enough to be a ballroom, huh?" Krystal jabbed.

Ballroom. That's the kind of music it was. All royal sounding, like we were about to witness a prince and princess have their first dance or something.

"That's right," Whit said, stepping back and lifting one arm up and the other arm out as if she was being held by someone. "Now, this is called the waltz." We all stood there looking at her like she had lost her mind as she lifted onto her tippy-toes and started counting, "One-two-three, one-two-three, one-two-three, one-two-three," moving robotically, back, then left, then front, then right, dancing in squares, the violins from the music whining in the background.

"What y'all waiting for?" Whit called out, stepping and sliding, her back stiff as a board.

"We waiting for you to stop," Krystal said.

"And I'm waiting on y'all to start," Whit threw right back, one-two-three-ing forward. I glanced over at the track. The other runners were doing their own thing, for the most part. The distance runners were working on pacing, the other eight-hundred runners were running fart licks, working on endurance, and the sprinters, well, specifically, Lu and Ghost, they were looking over at us, smirking. Ugh.

"You serious?" Brit-Brat was asking, already knowing the answer. As a matter of fact, she didn't even wait for Whit to answer and instead saved herself the frustration by being the trailblazer for the rest of us and getting in position. One arm up as if she was waiting for someone to grab it and arm wrestle her, and the other arm curved as if wrapped around the waist of somebody else. Someone with a rose in their mouth.

Krystal didn't follow.

Neither did Deja.

But me, I was new, and it didn't seem like a good idea to pop slick on one of the coaches. So I did what I had to do and became a real-life dance mannequin. As soon as I lifted my arm, I could feel Lu's and Ghost's snickers run down my spine, prickly like ice water. I didn't know if they really were laughing, but

I was pretty sure they were. And even if they weren't, I could feel them thinking about it.

"One-two-three, one-two-three." Coach Whit was still counting and pacing, ignoring the fact that Deja and Krystal were holding out.

"Just do it," Brit-Brat groaned at them. "So we can get it over with."

"I just don't see what this has to do with running," Deja said, reluctantly lifting her arms.

"I wanna tell you, but since y'all making me dance alone, I can't," Whit said, batting her eyes, laughter just under her tongue.

"Ugh." Krystal threw herself into a lazy karate stance.

"Very nice. Now ladies, follow me." And then, back to the one-two-three, one-two-three, except now we were following Whit's steps. Backward. Left. Forward. Right. One-two-three, one-two-three, one-two-three, one-two-three. *Four-five-six, seven-eight-nine, blah-blah-blah, blah-blah-blah,* I muttered to myself, betting that this was what the real fart lickers, Lu and Ghost, were saying to each other, their tongues hanging from their mouths like hounds, mimicking us (me) by doing the robot or something. And Aaron was probably saying something like, "You can't win first place being ballerinas," even though this wasn't even ballet. But he was probably right (if he was saying that). I, a second-place winner (loser), couldn't win first doing this. I didn't know what kind of training methods Whit had, or what discount aisle Coach found her in, but . . . dancing? Dancing?

"One-two-three, one-two-three. Very nice, girls," Whit said, all coachy like this was real practice. Then she sideswiped us. "Now, pair up."

"What?" Krystal stopped. Arms down. Head cocked.

"You always run when the gun goes off, so I know you ain't deaf, Krystal." Whit was clearly reaching the end of her patience rope. And I couldn't blame her. But I also couldn't blame Krystal for being snappy. This was wack. "Pair up. You're gonna dance with each other, and you can pout and suck your teeth and whatever else, but if you wanna win as a relay team . . ." Whit stopped dancing, folded her arms across her chest. "It's your call."

Well, no surprise here. I wanted to win. I really wanted to win, and straight up, if Whit told me that having my blood cleaned was the way to win, I would go to dialysis just like Ma. Now, I know that ain't the case. But I'd do it if it was.

I glanced over at Brit-Brat. Nodded. She turned

toward me and reached for my hand. "Let's just get it over with," she mumbled, facing me but directing her words to her fellow vets.

Krystal and Deja let out loud breathy huffs and positioned themselves in front of each other.

"Now, just like before, but this time guide each other. Trust each other." Whit took a pause, inhaled and lifted her arms as if she was conducting an orchestra, and started again with the count.

One-two-three.

Me and Brit-Brat took a step back. Back for Brit, forward for me. It was awkward.

"Same leg, same motion, same time," Whit instructed.

One-two-three.

Me and Brit-Brat moved left. It was a little smoother.

One-two-three.

Forward, which was actually backward for me. Not smooth at all. As a matter of fact, Brit-Brat stepped on my foot. Good thing she's light. Keep moving.

One-two-three. To the right. Decent.

And on and on, but every time we'd make the step forward (which was my step backward) Brit would crush me. Just squash my feet with hers, until finally I just couldn't take it no more.

"You think you could watch your feet, Brit?" I said, trying to be as nice as possible. I didn't want her to think I was coming at her or anything. I didn't need no drama. But I did need my toes. I mean, who can run with broken feet? When I said it, I braced myself for the quick, sharp tongue-lashing that I usually served up whenever somebody tried me.

"My bad," Brit-Brat said softly, which I have to admit, threw me for a loop. I guess I shouldn't have expected her to trip, especially since she was the first person to even give this whole dance thing a chance. "My feet are huge."

I looked down. Whoa. When most people say that, well, first of all, I'm only used to them being boys. Boys around Barnaby Terrace like David Hunter, who at ten years old wore a size ten shoe. My mother said he had feet like rowboats. And if that was the case, then Brit-Brat had yachts. *How you even run with those things?* I wanted to say.

"It's cool," is what I actually said.

One-two-three.

But it wasn't cool, because it kept happening. She would try to move them to the side, but they just . . . were everywhere. EVERYWHERE.

One-two-three.

One-two-three. *Ouch!*

I had to adjust. Started taking bigger steps back in hopes of steering clear of those floppers. And it worked, but then she adjusted to my adjustment and still caught my big toe. Argh!

"Very good, ladies. Now, I want you to take one step back. Hold your pose, but separate yourself from your partner," Coach Whit instructed, the song now fading out, a new one beginning. The sound of claps came from the other end of the track. I cringed, already knowing what was happening, but I had to look anyway. And there they were, Ghost and Lu, slapping their stupid hands together like clowns.

"Dancing with the stars, Patty!" Lu yelled out. And before I could say anything—and I was going to—Coach, like, *Coach* Coach, started laughing too. He had been working with the boys' relay on the field and was now walking toward Lu and Ghost, letting out the nastiest cackle ever. So loud and ridiculous that everyone stopped what they were doing to watch him. He laughed and laughed, slapping his knee and patting his chest and throwing his head back, all the way across the field until he reached Lu and Ghost up by the hundred-meter start line. He threw his arm around both of their shoulders. They were still chuckling.

Then Coach whispered something in Lu's ear. Then in Ghost's. And then they weren't smiling no more. Coach pulled away from them and took a few steps back. Ghost and Lu looked horrified. But then they faced each other, awkwardly, took each other by the hands, awkwardly, held each other (barely) around the waist, awkwardly, and did their version of the waltz. Whoa. I almost passed out, and I wasn't the only one. Everyone started losing it.

"C'mon, fellas, stay on beat. One-two-three, one-two-three," I yelled, snapping my fingers on count. Brit-Brat jumped right in, and so did Krystal and Deja. Even Whit joined us.

"One-two-three, one-two-three, one-two-three," we all chanted, eventually leading to everyone chanting, all the runners, even Sunny.

Then we were all singing, "ONE-TWO-THREE!" waving our arms around like conductors (I don't know why, it just seemed appropriate), watching Lu and Ghost waddle side to side like toddlers who had just pooped their pants.

"Okay, okay, ladies," Coach Whit cut us off, still laughing, and tried to wrangle us back in. "Let's refocus." We all regained our composure and tried to reposition ourselves for more waltzing. Just as we grabbed hands,

Coach Whit said, "We're gonna do the same thing, but this time, let go of each other's hands. Separate yourselves so that another person could fit between you."

"Wait," Krystal said, immediately winding up. Her arms went from around Deja to her own hips. "So now we gotta dance in threes? Well, if that's the case, I volunteer Deja to dance between them two." Krystal pointed at me and Brit-Brat.

"Krystal . . . no. Just . . ." Coach Whit was stuck, struck by Krystal's ridiculousness. "Could one of y'all explain, please?" Deja took on the task. Then we took our places again, but this time Brit and I were standing about a foot away from each other. We held our hands the same, and on Whit's count, danced the waltz once more.

"Back," Whit instructed. "Nice and smooth. Remember when you were closer, the pressure of your partner, knowing the steps, working and moving in unison."

"You like a hippie or something?" Deja asked.

"Focus," Whit said. "Might learn something."

"Doubt it," Krystal groused under her breath, but still loud enough for us to hear.

One-two-three.

"Left. Now, forward." I was happy—relieved—there was space between Brit and me. Space for her feet to meet ground, and not my toes. It was also kinda cool to see all four of us moving around, swaying and stepping all at the same time. Reminded me of the Olympics— the only thing I like to watch, besides running, are the synchronized swimmers. I mean, to move like that in the water is crazy. Cheerleaders do it too, sort of. But not like synchronized swimmers. And me, Brit-Brat, Deja, and Krystal (once she finally shut up) were like synchronized swimmers . . . uh . . . synchronized runners. Ah. Ahhhhhhhh. Sneaky, sneaky, Whit.

We had made like twenty or thirty squares before Whit, finally, thank you Lord, cut the music. "Okay, that's enough. Good job. So, how did it feel?" Then she pointed at Krystal, who was already fixing her mouth to crack a joke. Whit didn't say nothing to her. Just pointed, like, *Don't.*

"It felt weird at first," I spoke up.

"Yeah, definitely. And I kept stepping on Patty's feet," Brit admitted. "But then we kinda adjusted, y'know?"

"Right. Same for us. Like after a few times you just kinda stop thinking about it," Deja said.

Coach Whit looked at Krystal, who was smirking. "It was cool," she said with a shrug, eyes everywhere.

Coach Whit nodded, poked her bottom lip out,

not in the sad way, but in the surprised and satisfied way. "Well, let me ask you all this," a clever grin replacing the pokey-lip. "How many of you realized that I stopped counting a long time ago?"

The rest of practice was Whit giving us the rundown about the handoff—the passing of the baton—and how it was just like dancing the waltz, but we didn't actually practice it. She said we would be spending a portion of every practice for the rest of the week doing relay work; she was hoping that we'd be ready to give it a try by Saturday's meet.

I found out after practice that Krystal, Deja, and Brit-Brat had run relay last year, which is why they were so annoyed by the whole dance thing.

"I'm just sayin', it ain't that deep. You run, then you hand the stick to the next person. Then they run." That's pretty much exactly what I thought it was. "All this cha-cha mess was . . . I mean, it was fine, but it ain't necessary," Krystal complained afterward. She took a swig of water, then threw her bottle in her duffel bag, zipped it shut.

"The waltz," I corrected her, even though she was echoing my own feelings. It was cool, but it didn't really seem all that helpful. At least not yet. Krystal shot me a look, but I didn't pay it no mind because over her shoulder I could see Maddy coming toward me. Krystal went on mimicking the one-two-three count, Deja chiming in with the perfect amount of complementary snark, Brit-Brat laughing at them both.

"A'ight, I'll see y'all tomorrow."

"A'ight, Patty."

"Bye, Patty."

"Yo, Patty!" Ghost was just coming off the track, wiping his face with the bottom of his shirt. "You out?"

"Yeah."

"Without saying nothin'?" He cocked his head to the side. "So you ain't one of us no more? You too good for Sunny, Lu, and me?" He smiled, making it clear he was joking.

"Sunny's my guy. I love Sunny."

"Oh you love Sunny, but not me and Lu?"

"I mean . . ." At that moment, Maddy's arms wrapped around my waist. I could feel her rocking back, trying to get me to lift off my feet. I kissed her on the top of the head, immediately noticing fewer beads on her braids, which was normal. They fall off during the week like acorns from a tree. "Hey, hey." I tried to get her to stop squeezing. "Tell Momly I'm coming. First, say hi to Ghost." Maddy waved, then turned and ran back toward the car. Now, back to Ghost. "I mean . . . I wouldn't wanna get in the middle of y'all relationship."

"Stop."

"Dancing so sweetly with each other."

"Stop."

"So precious."

"I'm leaving." Ghost turned around and walked toward Lu, who was sitting on a bench, unlacing his track shoes.

"C'mon, Ghost. Ghost! Don't be that way!" I begged to his back.

"Bye, Patty." He threw his hand up, dismissing me.

"I love you, Ghost!" I shouted. "But just not as much as I love Sunny!" Of course, Sunny heard me, which I wasn't thinking about when I said it. We caught eyes, but I didn't wanna make it weird, or for him to think it was anything more than a joke, so I added, "Because you pay attention to details." Then held my hands up, spirit-finger style. "Thanks for noticing my Flo Jos. See you tomorrow."

TO DO: Eat turkey wings
(for the millionth day in a row)

THE RIDE HOME always goes like this:

Momly turns the radio news down, then asks how practice was. I tell her it was fine. She asks if I'm tired and even if I am, I tell her I'm not, just because I don't want Maddy to hear that I'm tired and think I won't be able to help her with stuff like her homework, which every day when I ask her about it, she tells me Momly already helped her, and before I can even say anything, Momly just says, "Didn't want you to have to worry about it," which I just nod at. Then I tell Momly I'll help her make dinner as soon as my homework's done, and she says, "I've already started cooking," and by then, Maddy's already started kicking the back of my seat for the rest of the ride, which drives me crazy, but also in some weird way, kinda relaxes me. Like a massage and a message—*I'm here, Patty. And I'm fine.*

And today was no different. I was tired. Acted like I wasn't. Maddy's homework was done, and I had a little left of mine to do before dinner. Nothing too major. I knocked out my math assignment. English homework was to think about cannons, which basically meant English homework was to think about history homework, which was going to be reading up more on Frida Kahlo so I could be ready to add some new information to our project. Not like anyone else was going to. I figured T-N-T and Becca were probably at home, I don't know, tanning or something. It wouldn't have surprised me if they had one of those skin cooker things in their houses. Those beds you lay on that come down over the top of you and roast you, and you come out looking like rotisserie chicken. Meanwhile, I was researching.

THINGS I LEARNED ABOUT FRIDA, so far:

(1) She was from Mexico.

(2) She was diagnosed with polio when

she was six, which made her right leg
skinnier than her left.

(3) When she was eighteen, she got into
a bus accident that broke her spine,
crushed her right leg and foot, and
made it impossible for her to have
babies. Doctors said she would never
walk again.

"Patty? Um . . . Patty?" A squeaky voice, way too
silly to be real, came from the other side of my bedroom door. Uncle Tony. He dropped the Daffy Duck
talk. "Dinner's almost ready. You almost done with
your homework?" My uncle's voice, when he's speaking like a regular human being, is deep, but not in a
scary way. He has one of those voices that you wish
you could touch, wrap yourself up in like a blanket.
A voice like a dad. And, I guess . . . like an uncle. A
favorite uncle.

Me and Uncle Tony been close for forever. He's
one of these big-kid grown-ups, a goof troop, all
jokes, all the time. And when I was younger, he was
one of the only people who could make my mom
laugh—like, a laugh that seem to come up from her
feet—after we lost my father. And up from her belly,

after she lost her feet. As a matter fact, he was one of the only people who could make any of us laugh back then.

"I'm almost done," I said, bookmarking the websites I'd been browsing. "Tell Momly I'll be right out to help." I jotted one last note. Something I'd read that I didn't think was that important to the project, but . . . maybe.

(4) Frida was close to her father.

And that, more than anything, was what me and Frida had in common. Only difference is, Frida's dad didn't die when she was young. So she didn't know what that was like. She didn't know what it felt like to be broken until she was older. And not only did I know the feeling of something breaking inside me, I also had to watch my mom go through it and basically get paralyzed in a whole different way. In her brain and in her heart. Matter of fact, after Dad passed, that's when Ma got all churchy-churchy. The beginning of catching the spirit and dancing in the aisle and "praying for peace in the eye of the storm."

But she had no idea the storm was just getting started, because that's also when she started eating.

Like, a lot. And not just regular food, but sweets. All my dad's favorite recipes. Sweet potato cheesecake and peanut butter brownies and white chocolate cookies and, of course, the delicious yellow cupcake with strawberry icing.

"Your daddy used to say this thing was so good they'd make you slap your mama," Ma would say, nibbling the top of the cupcake. "So you better not have too many of 'em."

We'd do like a ha-ha-ha, and then she'd have too too many of them. I guess maybe the sweets were a way of staying kinda connected to my dad. Dessert for the deserted. And I'm not gonna pretend like it wasn't amazing living in a house that always smelled like cooked sugar—which smelled like him. And heaven. It was great. But eventually, it wasn't. Because diabetes came and took Ma's legs. Took most of what was left of her laugh, too.

And that's when the actual storm reached maximum storminess. And I was pretty messed up by the whole thing, but doing my best to be strong and brave and big, and all the other things I ain't really feel like being at the time. I'd rather be sneaking lipstick on in the bathroom, sending Cotton selfies of how fly I looked, then washing it all off so my mother wouldn't see it. Or sitting on the curb at Cotton's, painting our nails with the nail polish I wasn't allowed to wear that her big brother, Skunk, would steal from the beauty store, even though I would have to scrub mine clean before I came back home unless it was clear polish, but then, what's the point? Or trying to convince my mother to let me use cucumber-mango or berry–rose water or kiwi-coconut or any other fruity-flowery good-smelling lotion on her swollen, cracked-up legs. Flipping through magazines, cringing at kitten heels, even though those were the only ones I ever had a shot of wearing in Bev Jones's house.

That's what I used to do, what I wanted to be doing, but I couldn't do none of those things no more. At least, not like I wanted to, because now I had to look out for Maddy, who was just . . . confused. I think she had just turned four, too young to really understand what was going on with Ma's health. And it was really hard to explain it all to her. So I told Maddy that Ma's legs had to . . . go away. Looking back on it, maybe it wasn't the best idea, but at the time it was all I had. And it seemed to help. And that's when that crazy thing I was talking about earlier, that crazy moment with Maddy, happened.

She asked me to help her write a letter. She said it

was for school, so of course, I grabbed a pencil and a sheet of paper from her backpack, set Maddy in the little chair at her desk, leaned over, and asked what she wanted the letter to say.

She wanted it to say this:

Dear Mommy legs,

I remember my hand instantly started shaking, and I was squeezing the pencil tight enough to snap it in half. But I kept writing what Maddy told me to write.

Where did you go, and why did you have to leave? And what are you doing? Are you having fun without us? Are you jumping? Are you dancing? Are you running fast? Please come back. We miss you.

Love,
Madison Jones

I dropped the pencil.

"Maddy, what . . . what you gon' do with this?" I tried to clear the shake from my voice, and it took me flexing every muscle in my body—even cracked my toes—just to keep the tears inside my face. Thank goodness her back was to me.

"First, I'm gonna bring it to school for show-and-tell."

"Oh . . . okay, um, and then what?"

"Well, after I show it to the class, I was gonna see if maybe you could send it."

"Send it?"

"To the legs." Maddy threw her head back, her big eyes staring up at me.

Hold it in, Patty. Hold it in. "Um . . . yeah, yes . . . I will . . . um, send it." I kissed her forehead.

"Your legs ain't gonna run away too, are they?" she asked, worry suddenly washing across her face.

"No, Maddy." I slapped my legs. "These ain't going nowhere."

"How you know?" she asked.

I didn't have a good answer to that, and instead toothed my bottom lip to keep it from quivering. "I just . . . I just do," I eked out, barely. "I'll prove it."

"How?" she asked. "How you gonna prove it?"

"Well . . . I don't know, but I'll figure it out." *Don't say it, Patty. Don't say it.* "I promise." I said it. And instantly felt like I messed up. Like I said something wrong. I wished I had had an invisible cupcake to stuff in my mouth. Something. Some stupid pretend tea. Anything. I mean, how was I going to prove my legs weren't going to run away from me? Would this be one of those things I was going to have to hope Maddy just forgot about? But the pressure of it all was worth it, because the worry on Maddy's face unwound.

She nodded, then hit me with the gut punchiest of all gut punches. "Pinky promise?" Oh . . . no. Pinky promises, for us, ain't no joke. They're like contracts. Break a pinky promise and people will make you feel like you in jail or something. Friendship jail, or in this case, big sister jail.

Maddy held her pinky out. I hooked mine onto hers, touched thumbs. Now she knew there was no way I would let her down. Then she got back to business. She tapped the letter. "So, you know where to send this?" she followed—blow after blow after blow. Killing me, Waffle. But this one, I couldn't answer. At all. I just couldn't. So I just left, ran to my room, threw myself on the bed, and curled into a ball. *Breathe, Patty. Breathe.*

Crazy thing was, the next day at school we were having a field day, and I was paired on a relay race team with Lu. I know I said I never ran one, but this wasn't like a real relay. This was more just slapping each other's hands and running as fast as we could. And after our race, it was Lu who told me about his track club he was in at the time—the Sparks. That night, I went home and asked Uncle Tony and Momly, and all the dots connected. My first club team. The rest, as they say, is history. Or . . . present. All I know is it just seemed like something somewhere (um . . . legs don't got souls, right?) was telling me to do it. Pushing me to do it. Not just for me. But for Dad. And for Ma. And for Maddy, who (bonus!) I suddenly—thankfully—had an answer for. Pinky promise and all.

Turkey wings. Momly made turkey wings every single night. Every. Single. Night. So it's always funny because when Uncle Tony says things like, "Dinner's almost ready," I never have to ask what we having. I know what we having. Turkey wings. With rice and a veggie. Usually broccoli. Not even turkey breast, or a turkey leg, or even a turkey sandwich. Wings only. I had never had them before we came to live with them, and the first night Momly cooked them I told her I liked them, and that was it. It was set in stone. Turkey wings for life.

Momly kept the kitchen just like she kept the car. Clean. Germ free. Scrubbed from top to bottom with something sudsy and bright colored, like sun yellow that smelled like rotten lemon, or mutant green that smelled like if every flower in the world sneezed. I pulled up to the table; Maddy was peeling fat off the meat. Cauliflower tonight. White broccoli. But not nearly as white as the spotless dinner plates.

After I told Momly what I had to tell her every night, which was that I was sorry for not finishing my homework in time to help her, she kicked off the dinner small talk with telling us about her favorite patient. See, she got her own business (but it don't make her boat money) where she takes care of sick people—Emily's Expert Care, which I think is a terrible name, by the way. Ain't got no warmth to it. No hug in it. I think it should be called something like, In Emily's Arms, or Mobile Mom. Something like that. Maddy thinks it should be called Momly to the Rescue, and, well, even though I don't like that name either, it would at least be a true statement. At least for Ma, because when me and Maddy went to go live with Momly and Uncle Tony, it just made sense for Momly to add Ma to her client list, along with the most-talked-about of them all, Mr. Warren, who Momly calls the sweetest old man alive. But I don't really know if my mother is the sweetest old lady alive, and Ma wasn't really happy about none of it at first, just because she don't really like nobody taking care of her. But at least it's family and not some stranger, even though she can definitely, uh . . . be a lot to deal with. Actually, now that I think about it, maybe a stranger would've been better. I bet during those first few visits, Ma almost drove Momly to Jesus too. Or off a cliff.

"Well, my favorite patient besides your mother," Momly clarified about Mr. Warren. He was an old man who had Alzheimer's, which basically just means he can't really remember too much no more. She said sometimes random stuff popped into his head, but usually he doesn't know where he is, even though he's in his own house. So he just stays in the bed now. And Momly goes over there and feeds him, and makes sure he's all cleaned up while his daughter runs around taking care of errands and stuff. Momly's been looking out for him for a long time.

"I went to use the bathroom, and when I got back to the room, he was up out of the bed, tearing the room apart looking for something. He was yanking clothes out of the closet, and snatching pictures off the wall. So I asked him what he was looking for and he said, 'Something to buff the floor with.'"

"Buff the floor?" Uncle Tony asked. I was just as confused.

"That's what he said. And when I told him the floor didn't need buffing, he explained that he had mouths to feed, and who was going to take care of his family?" Momly laid her napkin in her lap, all proper, like she was eating in front of folks she ain't know. "Eventually I got him to calm down. Got him back in the bed, where he seemed to just melt back into himself. And I put everything back in the closet, and hung the pictures back on the wall." She shook her head. "Just one of those days. Poor guy." Momly took a breath, then turned to me. "Speaking of pictures on the wall, Patty, how's the whole Frida thing going?" Momly now pushed her fork through one of the tiny trees. Tired seemed to sit in her cheeks, make her face look saggy. It wouldn't have surprised me if she fell asleep right there at the table. "It's Frida, right?"

I nodded. I'd asked her if she knew anything about Frida when we first got the assignment, but she said she didn't. She had seen her in pictures, but that was pretty much it.

"It's goin' okay," I told her. "She seemed like a cool lady."

"But not as cool as you," Uncle Tony said, wiggling

his eyebrows. I wasn't sure if Momly was done small-talking me about my school project, but if she wasn't, Uncle Tony definitely ended any chance of it continuing because he awkwardly made a hard left into a totally different conversation. "Um . . . how was practice?"

Frida to track practice? Worst transition of all time. This is why Momly's the small-talk queen, and Uncle Tony's the cartoon character.

But I knew Uncle Tony wasn't trying to be rude, and that his jumpiness was all about my second-place loss at the meet on Saturday, which, by the way, he wasn't at. Had an emergency at the office. He does something called Information Technology, which is IT for short, or "it" for even shorter (which is what he says), which all just means he works with computers. And apparently sometimes computers have emergencies. Anyway, all this weird dinnertime chat was his way of knocking on the door of my brain, like, *Hey, is it okay to come in?* And if it wasn't for practice today, maybe I'd still be mad. I told him and Momly and Maddy about being chosen for the 4x800 relay team, and doing the waltz.

"The waltz? Like . . . the ball-gown, pinky-in-the-air dance?" Pinky-in-the-air was Uncle Tony's way of saying fancy.

"Yep. It was to teach us something about being in tune with each other. Like knowing each other so well that we don't even have to think about the handoff."

"Maddy, sweetheart, eat your cauliflower," Momly's exhausted voice slid between me and Uncle Tony's.

Maddy groaned. "Eat your cauliflower," I repeated. "It'll make you strong." Uncle Tony, following my lead, curled his arms up, making his muscles jump. Maddy smiled.

"Well, if doing the waltz is all it takes, then let me show you how to run even faster," Uncle Tony said. Then, as soon as he said it he braced himself, thinking I would catch feelings, as if I thought he was saying I don't run fast enough, and judging by Saturday, I don't. Not fast enough. But it was cool.

"Uncle Tony, I'm not mad no more," I told him, getting straight to the point so he could stop acting so weird.

His shoulders dropped, rolled back as if he just unbuttoned the top button on his pants after a big meal. "Oh, thank God," he exhaled the words, and I smirked, then tapped my fork on Maddy's plate. She stabbed a piece of cauliflower, lifted it to her mouth. Uncle Tony continued, "So, yeah, if you wanna run faster, try this."

He scooted out from the table, Momly already frowning at whatever was coming. And then . . . it came. The strangest thing I've seen Uncle Tony do, maybe ever. The Running Man. Spastic and offbeat and all over the place.

Maddy busted out laughing, white mush in her mouth, and I was right behind her, my laughter scrubbing away the last 10 percent of sad in me. Uncle Tony lurched forward, pumping his legs, panting, "This . . . is . . . how . . . you . . . do . . . it . . . Patty . . . ," and I kept snickering. My uncle, a straight-up clown.

7

TO DO: Calm down, count to ten
(or ten thousand)

THE FIRST THING I do in the morning every Monday, Wednesday, and Friday is send Ma a text message of a smiley face, just to let her know I'm thinking about her on the days she has to get her blood cleaned. And when I say cleaned, I don't mean cleaned like scrubbed. You try to scrub blood, you just gonna wind up with nasty red hands. What I mean by cleaned is the doctors do this thing where they run the blood out of one of her veins through a tube that's connected to a machine, and that machine takes all the bad stuff out, and then pumps the blood out of the other end through a different tube and back into a different vein. Takes like three or four hours, and leaves her super tired, but she gotta do it because the sugar also broke her kidneys, and when your kidneys don't work, your blood gets dirty. And when your blood gets dirty, it basically messes all kinds of other stuff up inside you. Think about it like this: When you get dirt in your shoe, do it feel good? Nope. It makes you walk with a limp, like there are little fires blazing between your toes. And when you get dirt in your eye, can you see? Of course not. And it burns like crazy, too, every little speck of dirt like a teeny-tiny lit match. So imagine having dirt in your blood. Mess your whole body up. Make your organs feel like they in a microwave.

So, yeah, I text her to let her know I'm thinking about her on those days. I text her on other days too, but especially on the blood-cleaning days. She always sends a smiley face back, which I appreciate because I know how much she hates texting. She loves getting them, but really hates sending them.

Momly is who goes to pick Ma up, who takes her to the hospital's dialysis—another word with "die" in it—unit, where she gets the treatment, who then brings her back home. And because Momly gets to Ma's house at the butt crack of dawn, Ma goes to bed dumb early on Sundays, Tuesdays, and Thursdays so she can be up and ready to go. And whenever Ma's not at treatment, she's recovering from it, which means she's usually lying in bed drifting in and out of sleep watching TV, or as she always puts it, "letting the TV watch her." So the morning smiley faces we send each other are important.

Correction: the smiley faces we send to each other are important to *me*. Almost as important as Vicky Tines's boyfriend is to Vicky Tines, who she announces is in high school every single day in homeroom. Mrs. Stansfield takes roll by going down her list and looking to see who's there and who's not. At Barnaby, Ms. Simmons used to call our names out loud. Needed to hear our voices. But in homeroom at Chester, there were a lot of voices already being heard. Like Vicky Tines's. Ugh. All of Vicky's friends be having heart eyes when they listen to Vicky go on and on (and on and on and on). Macy Franks pays no attention to her and just folds paper. Like, what's the name of that thing . . . that way you fold paper into animals and all that? Mrs. Richardson used to help me and Cotton make paper fortune-tellers when she was babysitting us back in the day. Used to give mine to Momly when she picked me up. But my fortune-teller ain't never predict this, that's for sure. Anyway, Macy just be doing that. Making birds and stuff. Laurie Brenner wants a belly-button ring. Jasmine Stanger already got one. I saw it when she was showing Laurie. Pretty sure something's wrong with it.

First period, English. Mr. Winston is teaching us poetry. Which means Mr. Winston is teaching us boredom. My uncle said, "Tell Mr. Winston to teach y'all some Queen Latifah." At Chester? Right. Remember the whole "think about cannons" thing? That's because we've been learning this one called "The Charge of the Light Brigade." Cannons are mentioned in it, and Mr. Winston reads it like he some kind of actor or something, all bass-y and slow, like the man who narrates the previews at the movies. Like his dramatic voice is gonna make the poem any less wack. But hot sauce on cardboard is still cardboard.

Then comes math. Geometry. Ms. Teller says "perpendicular" and "hypotenuse" like her life depends on it. My life depends on math being over as quickly as possible.

Then lunch.

Okay, I know what you're thinking, what you think I'm gonna say. You think I'm gonna go on some kind of rant about how the cafeteria is basically like some kind of "meanie mealtime" and little ol' Patty Watty doesn't have a group so she can't find a seat, right? Wah wah wah! Right? Well . . . right. Kinda. But not exactly. See, the real issue with the cafeteria is that it's tiny. Like teeny-tiny. It's almost as if when they started this academy, they didn't expect there to be so many people who would actually come to get academied. They probably never thought regular kids from regular neighborhoods and regular schools would end up here. But here I am. Looking for a seat in a space as small as the church we go to, and with just as much noise, but none of the spirit.

Point is, there was never enough seats, which was okay, because I never sat down anyway. I would basically just do a few laps around the room, scarfing my pasta Bolognese, which I found out was not pasta and baloney, but was actually just regular spaghetti. But yeah, I'd just circle the room, because when you keep moving, people think you going somewhere, like you on a mission and shouldn't be bothered. Like you busy. And that's better than people realizing that you not busy at all. That you not okay with lunchrooms that don't have trays, and that ain't big enough spaces to disappear in, and that don't stink of week-old dirty mop water, which I now know is the familiar smell of love and friendship.

Usually, on the tenth lap, my food would be gone, and the bell would ring. I had it all timed perfectly. But today, on lap number two, barely into my salmon teriyaki, which, by the way, should be called teriyaki salmon the same way barbecue chicken is barbecue chicken and not chicken barbecue. I swear . . . Chester. Anyway, on lap two, Becca stood up from her seat like a bird who just popped its head out of a nest, and waved at me. Well, not at me, but she waved me over. And I felt . . . funny. Like, confused, and weirded out, and skeptical, and yes, I can't front, a little excited. I cut between the tables, holding my plate steady, and once I got to where she was, smack in the middle of a crowded table full of . . . well . . . you know . . . girls on either side of her eating and talking and laughing, she said, "What are you doing?"

"What you mean?" I replied, pretending like I hadn't just been acting like a lunch monitor, trying not to drop my plate while forking my fish.

"I mean, how come you're not sitting?" she asked. The girl beside her, a girl I'd seen every day but never really met, whipped her face toward me. Two faces looking at mine. Four rosy cheeks. Four mascaraed eyes. Four bazillion strands of blond.

"Oh, I'm good."

"But you never sit," Becca pressed. "Like . . . ever."

And before I could either drop my plate, or say anything, Becca bumped the girl next to her, who then bumped the girl next to her, who bumped the girl next to her who happened to be Macy Franks, folding her teriyaki streaked plate into a Styrofoam half-moon. They all scooted over, squishing together, making a sliver of free space on the seat. Was this some kind of joke? A trick? A scheme for Becca to milk me for info about Frida or something? Either way, I was tired of eating standing up, so I set my plate down, slowly climbed over the bench, and slipped my legs under the table. Then, as if none of this was a big deal, Becca turned back to her conversation—a ditzy discussion about music in space—and I turned back to my salmon teriyaki. Yeah. Kinda awkward.

After lunch it was time for my favorite girl group. I mean, history. Ms. Lanford was standing at the board, chewing the last bit of her lunch, as we all filed in and took our seats in our assigned-group clusters.

"Don't forget to figure out when you're going to meet outside of class to work on this. Not everything can be done in school." Ms. Lanford wiped crumbs from the corners of her mouth. Looked like she may have had crackers for lunch. Definitely not salmon teri-yaki. "Hopefully, today everyone is prepared to share with their partners some more new findings about the person you all have chosen."

"Hey," I said first, scooting my chair up to the desk. T-N-T sort of spoke back. Sometimes their hi's sounded more like humphs. But only to me. Their hi's to Becca came with weird no-touch hugs. But whatever.

"Hey, Patina." Becca beamed, much warmer than the other two girls. As if I hadn't just been sitting next to her at lunch. She pulled out the materials we put together yesterday. Well, really, the stuff I put together. The photos of Frida I found on Google. Then the three of them looked at me like I had something magical to say.

I returned the stare. Blank face.

"So . . . anything new we should know about . . . um . . ." TeeTee started but couldn't remember Frida's name.

"Frida."

"Yeah, Frida. Anything new we should know about her?" She cocked her head to the side. I imagined her brain oozing out of her ear.

"You tell me." Me = running out of patience.

"I watched the movie about her online last night,"

Becca blurted out, all excited. "Um, well, I watched some of it. There's Spanish in it, and that threw me off. But I saw the part where she was in school and on the bus with her boyfriend, who by the way was hot, just saying, and the bus got in an accident and gold dust went everywhere and the next thing you know, Frida is just lying there all bloody. A mess. And then she's got a cast over her whole body. She painted butterflies on the cast after the cute boyfriend moved to Europe, which I was like, what? No! So . . . yeah."

T-N-T turned their attention back toward me to see if Becca was right. As if I was some kind of expert on gold dust, butterflies, and blood.

"That's wassup, Becca," I said, smiling, nodding. "But there's some details you left out." Here's the thing. At this point, I had already come to grips with the fact that this group project was going to be a Patty project. Ms. Lanford told us at the very beginning that there would be one grade given, so everybody had to do a fair share. But how in the world was I supposed to tell the T(a/e)ylors to get it together? How was I supposed to say, *Yo, I ain't doing all the work?* I guess I could've just said it like that, but I didn't want no static. I didn't want to be on nobody's bad side, especially since I wasn't even really on nobody's good side yet. Matter of fact, I wasn't on nobody's side, period.

Man, I missed Cotton.

I know that's such a random thought, but in moments like these, I missed her bad. And what made it worse was that I couldn't even talk to her, because Barnaby Middle was on spring break like everybody else—Chester's was the next week—and her grandma took her on their annual cruise trip, which Cotton don't even like because she says she don't do nothing but sit around with no cell phone service, eating shrimp all day and looking out at all the water she can't swim in while her granny plays slot machines. But if Cotton was here, if she was in this group with me, she would've just made up all types of silly stories. Oh, Frida? She was the first woman in Mexico to go to the NFL. Oh, Frida? She invented the flute. Used to play with James Brown and them. Oh, Frida? She's the first woman to have a day named after her—Friday. By the way, Thursday was named after Thurgood Marshall. That's Cotton. She would've turned everything into a joke until T-N-T realized it wasn't. That none of this was. That this was about a . . . number . . . grade. A four. I needed a four. Even if that meant I had to do three other people's work to get it.

I pulled out my notebook and started running

down more facts about Frida, filling in some of Becca's holes. "She also went to one of the top schools in Mexico. It was probably like this one." Becca nodded. She was in. The other two were still holding out. I tried one more time to make a connection. "And that's where she met Diego Rivera, who at the time was painting a mural in the school auditorium."

"That's the fat man, right?" Becca interjected, excited to share more of what she must've seen in the movie. But it came off kinda mean, so she added, "I mean . . . I didn't mean it like that. But that's him, right?"

"Right. And what's really interesting is she ended up marrying him once she healed from the accident. Not right away, but a few years after."

"The fat man," TeeTee chimed in, just to confirm that we were still talking about the same Diego. "What did he look like?"

Becca sifted through the papers until finding one with his picture, and stabbed his face with her finger. "Him."

"Him? She could've done better than him. And he looks so old," Taylor scoffed.

"He was old. Twenty years older," I explained. Taylor leaned forward, the drama of that kind of relationship seeming to send some kind of electrical charge through her. Suddenly, Frida was a little more interesting.

TeeTee pinched the corner of a picture of Frida, the one where her neck is too long and a small monkey's looking over her shoulder, and turned the picture around.

"I mean, she wasn't like . . . she definitely coulda done better than that guy," she said, studying Frida's face.

"Yeah, I agree. But he was a genius with a paintbrush, and I guess that's why she chose him. People used to call their relationship 'the Elephant and the Dove.'"

Becca's eyes lit up. "Like Beauty and the Beast!"

Taylor grimaced. "I guess," she said, and just then it occurred to me that we were all leaning in, analyzing Frida's and Diego's faces, looking through the pictures, discussing something . . . interesting. Sure, it was about their crazy love story, but still. It was a start. And if it weren't for the piercing sound of the fire alarm suddenly going off, we might've been able to get to some of the other cool things about Frida Kahlo, but at least we decided whose house we would go over to do the "go over somebody's house" portion of the project. Becca's. Taylor and TeeTee basically begged Becca to host it at her place, which I guess made sense because it was right across the street from the school. Becca said the best day to do it at her house would be the next day, Wednesday, because her grandmother was making cookies, which T-N-T said was perfect because Thursday was Taylor's mother's birthday, and Friday . . . was Friday. I told them I could do it, but I'd have to come by after track practice, and if it wasn't for the alarm suddenly screaming over us, maybe, just maybe, they would've asked about my running. But I guess fire drills are important too.

At least they are to six-year-olds.

Specifically six-year-olds named Madison Jones.

"But just in case there is a real fire, it's good we practice, right?" Maddy went on and on in the car after school. From the moment I met her in the hallway she'd been blabbing, so excited about the hustle and bustle she'd experienced earlier in the day. Fire drill, fire drill, fire drill. It's like that was the only thing that happened in the north wing of Chester.

"I think we should also maybe practice stop, drop, and roll with Mrs. S," Maddy barreled on, rolling her hands in the air. "Just in case somebody don't make it out in time, especially since she make us all walk so slow. I don't know about everybody else, but if there's a for-real fire, I'm outta there."

Momly snorted.

"But what about me?" I asked.

Maddy thought about it for a second. "Patty, I can lift you up, but I don't think I can lift you and run."

"Not yet," I replied, sliding one arm out of my shirtsleeve.

"Right. Not yet." Maddy flexed one of her arms, squeezed her bicep.

The ride to MLK Park was the one thing that got Maddy to stop yakking about fire drills . . . for some reason she still geeked out at the fancy houses we passed on the way, especially the big white ones, their wooden castle doors with knobs like golden fists. The fountains and wraparound driveways. The windows— no curtains, like they want everybody to know what they got. But can't nobody really see nothing any- way, because of the gates, the tops of the metal posts curling up into the air like witch fingers. And in front of the gates, shrubs. And then the mailbox, with the address, which is always just one or two numbers. Like 6 Chester Ave. Or 13 Chester Place. And as we moved through town, the numbers continued to climb as the neighborhoods changed. From mansions to weird cereal-box communities, where every house looks like a different version of the one next to it. Then on to older neighborhoods like mine, where the houses are still nice, but have been around for a while, so still made of brick. My address has three numbers. 685 Wallery Street. But Ma's address, over in Barnaby Terrace, has four—5014. And I think Ghost's is something like five or six. It's like the less numbers in your bank account, the more numbers in your address.

Practice was a little less silly today. Well, it got less silly after warm-up laps, stretching, and the usual clowning around. Well, Lu was clowning Curron.

"Yo, Curron, how come yesterday Coach ain't make y'all do that dancing thing Patty and Krystal did?" he asked, winding up and tossing a live grenade into the mix. He had one of his legs pulled back behind him, doing a final stretch.

"You mean what he made you and Ghost do?" Curron jabbed. "Because we don't need all that on the boys' relay," Curron bragged, cutting his eyes at Brit-Brat.

"Oh, y'all don't?" That was Krystal's cue to jump in. Brit-Brat didn't pay it no mind, and neither did I, because Curron was always trying us. Deja bucked a little, but Krystal beat her to it. "You do know that you can't keep taking off early in a relay race, right?

If you jump the gun more than once, y'all shot . . . is shot." Krystal laser-eyed Curron. "And everybody know you a gun-jumpin' fool." We all laughed. Everyone but Sunny, who was chillin', trapping his laughter in his face, as usual, so nobody knew what he was really thinking. Krystal moved closer, put her hand on Curron's shoulder like a concerned parent. "Seriously, is there gonna be one race where you don't false start?"

Everybody laughed again, but Curron didn't find it funny at all.

"Seriously, Krystal No-Speed, is there gonna be one day that your breath don't smell like boiling track shoes?" Curron slapped a hand over his nose. He zinged her with that one, and even though it was super petty, all of us were yikes-ing from the blowback. Then he turned to Ghost. "And I know you ain't laughin', Ghost. Maybe you need more practice with your dance partner, because you ran the whole race before you realized nobody was running with you. The. Whole. Race."

Ouch. I can't front, just thinking of Lu and Ghost holding each other like that made me want to burst into laughter. But I held it in. But not everyone did, the loudest coming from Aaron, Freddie, and Mikey, who all began fake-waltzing.

"Whatever! It was his first race! His . . . first . . . race!"

Lu came to Ghost's defense. And I was right there for the follow-up.

"Ever," I dropped in to drive home the point.

"Nah, it's cool," Ghost said, calling off his newbie goons. "How 'bout this, Curron. How 'bout you pick the distance, and we line up and—"

"Okay, okay, knuckleheads," Coach cut him off, sauntering over, swinging his stopwatch. "Let's get done with the funnin' so we can get down with the runnin'. I swear if you all could move your legs as fast as you move your lips, we wouldn't even have to practice." Time for Coach's daily pep talk.

"We got three practices left before the next meet. Today, tomorrow, and Thursday. Then it's go time. If you came here to play around"—he looked at Lu, the instigator—"when Saturday comes, don't cry when I don't run you. If you came to be lazy, I'll make sure you have a comfortable seat this weekend at the meet. Are we clear?" We all nodded. "It's Technique Tuesday. I watched some of your forms break down last week, out there looking like wet noodles. I don't wanna see that this week. Let's keep it tight." He tucked his elbows in, stuck his chest out. "Keep your stride wide, and remember to breathe. Come off the block like you got a point to prove." Coach then told the relay teams what Coach

Whit had already told us at the last practice—that we would also be working on baton passing. Thankfully, he didn't mention dancing.

Me, Brit-Brat, Krystal, and Deja went off to one end of the track with Coach Whit. She was holding small orange cones. Not the kind that you see at construction sites, or in school cafeterias whenever there was a spill. These were small. Where the heck do you even get such tiny cones? If Maddy saw them, she'd want them for pretend megaphones.

"Okay, ladies, I need you all to pay attention, because what I'm gonna show you could make or break you," she said.

Then Whit placed one of the cones just before the curve on the track, and another, I don't know, maybe twenty feet into the curve. "This is the handoff zone," she said, coming back from the second cone. "Or as Coach calls it, the hot zone. This is the amount of space you have to hand off the baton. Now, I know the three of y'all"—Whit pointed to Krystal, Deja, and Brit-Brat—"are used to standing at the starting line with your arm out waiting for the stick, but this year Coach and I have decided to shake things up. You're going to run the eight-hundred relay as if it were a one hundred relay."

jason reynolds

We looked at Whit like she had grown a second head. Once she realized that none of us understood what she was talking about, she explained, "What I mean is, we're gonna do blind handoffs."

"Wait, what you mean, blind?" Deja asked.

"Now she 'bout to blindfold us, y'all," Krystal joked.

"No, I'm about to show y'all how to win. That is, if you can shut up and listen. Especially you, Krystal, seeing as though you run the slowest leg." Krystal sucked her teeth, burned. Probably would've sucked her teeth hard enough to turn her whole face inside out if she could.

"Now, watch and learn," Whit said, and started demonstrating the blind handoff, a technique that usually only sprinters do during relays because of the momentum of the incoming runner. The runner who's receiving the baton has to time it exactly right, start sprinting before the runner with the baton reaches the line. So there's no slowdown.

"This is why I had you dance, ladies," Coach Whit was saying, moving Krystal and me to imaginary positions on the track. "Now, Krystal, you're coming in fast."

"Wait, we're running the eight hundred, not the four hundred," Brit-Brat said.

"So?"

"So . . . I mean, how fast do you really expect us to be coming in? By the time I get to the final stretch, I'm rigged. This is the hardest race to run," Brit-Brat argued, her arms spread wide, as if, what the? I nodded, thinking the exact same thing. The eight hundred ain't no dash.

"As fast as you possibly can. Our job is to run to win. If that means you have to run until your legs detach from your body, then that's what you do." Whit's face went dead serious. "Because the rest of your relay team is depending on you. Got it?" Brit nodded sheepishly. So did I. Coach Whit wasn't playing no games today.

"So, Krystal, pretend you're coming in, final stretch," Coach Whit gave Krystal the baton, stood beside her. "You want to line your right arm up with Patty's left shoulder. Now, whoever's receiving has the hard job, because they have to time the transition. In this case, it's Patty. When you see Krystal about to enter the red zone, where this cone is, you gotta take off, full speed. If you wait too long, you two will collide and get jumbled. If you go too early, the person passing the baton won't be able to catch up to hand it off. Make sense?" We all nodded.

"Now," she went on, "what this means for the

incoming runner is that you have to dig deep and run with everything you got on that final stretch, because once you yell out, 'Stick!' you still have to run fast enough to catch the next runner, who will have her arm out, but will also have fresh legs. So we all have to feel each other out. Know when to go. Know when to hand off. It's waltzing without touching. Just moving in rhythm. Now let's run it slow-mo a few times."

Coach Whit moved Krystal back twenty more feet and told her to jog toward me. Once Krystal got to the first cone, I started jogging. "Good," Coach Whit said. "Now call it!"

"Stick," Krystal said, no oomph behind it.

"No." Whit thrust her arm out across the Krystal's body like Momly does to me after slamming on the brakes. "I said, call it. Not say it." Whit took the baton and stepped back a few feet. "Stick! Stick!" she shouted, running toward us. "People are going to be screaming. You need to make sure your teammate hears you. Now, run it again."

When "stick" is called out, my job is to stretch my left arm behind me, without looking, while running full speed until Krystal slaps the baton in my hand. It's tricky, because our running has to match up. She has to have enough juice and enough time to get to me.

We ran it again and again, faster and faster, working on the timing of it all. Deja had to practice the handoff to Brit-Brat, and Brit-Brat had to practice the handoff to Krystal.

"Now remember, these cones won't be on the track. So you're gonna have to learn to eyeball when the transition should happen," Whit said, picking them up. "This time, full speed. Run it."

She told Deja to start back at the two-hundred-meter mark, outside lane, and do the handoff to Brit-Brat. It wasn't bad. Then she had Brit-Brat do the same to practice the handoff to Krystal.

"Stickstickstickstick!" was Brit-Brat's way of calling out, which made us all laugh, even Whit. But, hey, whatever works. Next it was my turn to receive the handoff from Krystal, but when she reached the red zone, and I broke out running, she couldn't catch me.

"Try it again," Whit said. So we did, and I got out too far ahead of her again. I wasn't trying to, but she's just . . . slower.

"Yo, what you tryna do?" Krystal asked, panting.

"What you talkin' 'bout? I'm waiting on you to call it out," I explained.

"No, you tryna play me," she said. "You over-running."

"Over-running? That ain't even a thing. Maybe you under-running—"

Coach Whit cut us off. "You two, cut it out and get back on your mark. Save that drama for the other teams on Saturday."

But Krystal wasn't ready to be cut off. Maybe it was because Curron snapped on her and Whit threw her a little shade earlier, but now Krystal was fuming. "Nah. See, I try to be nice to the new girl"—she looked around at Brit and Deja, all fired up—"but she always correcting me. And being all goody-goody, like she think she better than us." She raised her chin at me. "What make you better? Your white mother?"

My white . . . mother? Ohhhh . . .

"What?" My left eye twitched, a sign that things were going to go bad if Krystal didn't shut up. Nobody had ever tried to call me out about Momly before. Nobody had the nerve to even pretend to know something they really ain't know nothing about. Until now.

"You heard me." Krystal didn't shut up.

"Enough." Coach Whit slid between us, but that wasn't enough to stop what was coming. Because now I wasn't shutting up.

"I don't think I'm better than y'all. I think I'm better than you." I jabbed a finger over Coach Whit's shoulder right at Krystal. "And not because of no so-called white mother. But because I'm actually . . . better . . . than . . . you. I just am. You run like your feet made of oatmeal. Like your whole life is in slow-mo. I'm faster, because I work harder while you sit around and pout like some spoiled brat. Like somebody owe you ribbons. Like it's our job to carry your lazy—"

"Patty! THAT'S ENOUGH!" Whit yelled, whirling around to face me.

"Better watch who you playin' with," I snarled at Krystal, last dig in.

"PATTY, I SAID THAT'S ENOUGH!" Coach Whit grabbed me by the arm and dragged me off the track to the gate. My heart was pounding so hard that my chest felt like it had stopped pumping blood and was pushing those red beads I put in Maddy's hair through my veins instead. "Are you serious?" Whit asked when we were out of earshot. "What was that?"

I glared over at Krystal. Made sure she knew I wasn't scared. But I didn't answer Whit. Didn't want to, because if I did I would've said that that was me offering Krystal a seat and that she better take it before I showed her what it meant to lay down. I was so mad. So mad. White mother? I'm the daughter of Bev Jones. And she don't make no junk. Momly ain't even my real mother, but even if she was . . . what? I lasered in on Krystal's face. Her eyes, tearing up, her tough, tearing down. *You don't even know what you talkin' about, over there about to cry. What you about to cry for? You started it. Why you even have to go there? Why?*

"You hear me talking to you, Patty?"

I glanced at Coach Whit. "Yeah." I closed my eyes for a second, told myself to get a grip. Deep breaths, Patty, my mad slowly mellowing. This temper ain't a new temper. Breaking invisible teacups. Smashing them everywhere. No, this ain't new. I just be keeping it pushed down, all the way down in my legs. See, there was this weird period between my dad's passing and my mother losing her legs that my mom always calls "the funky zone" because I was acting, well . . . funky. Temper on a billion. As soon as somebody started with me—even if they looked like they wanted to start—I would finish it. Talk people down. Talk them out of whatever they thought they wanted with me. And I was just trying to let Krystal know, that's all. But it had been a long time since I had to get funky. And now that I had—and now that I noticed Krystal was really hurt—the "funk" was fading.

"So then I need you to answer me," Whit pressed, steely. "What was that?"

"Look, I'm sorry," I said, feeling somewhere between embarrassed and satisfied. But then I looked over at Krystal pretending I ain't cut her deep, doing her best to hold in her tears. Deja and Brit-Brat pretending like they minding their business but really they being nosy, watching us.

And . . . I felt bad. A little bit bad. I didn't want to, but . . . I did.

"What's going on here?" Coach had now made his way over to us.

"I'll let Patty tell you," Whit said, her voice still furious, stalking off to go talk to Krystal.

"It's nothing," I said quickly.

"Nothing?" Coach looked down at my hands. "Since when does 'nothing' make you look like you're about to punch somebody?"

I guess the funk hadn't completely faded yet.

I looked Coach in the eye but didn't say nothing. He mumbled something like, *I'm getting too old for this* under his breath. Then he startled me by shouting, to everyone, "Y'know, I'm not your daddy. I'm not your teacher, or your principal, or even your friend. I'm your coach. Your coach! My job is to coach you, to hopefully make you all better runners, but more importantly, better people!" He closed his eyes. "Krystal,

Deja, Brit-Brat, right here." He pointed to the ground in front of him. When they all came over, he took the baton from Krystal.

"Take one end," he ordered. I grabbed it, thinking this was going to be a revisit of the whole "energy of the team" speech. "Krystal, you take the other." She took the other end of the baton, looking like it was the last thing in the world she wanted to do. "If either of you let go, you're both off the team." Then he looked at Deja and Brit-Brat. "If you two see either one of them let go, you tell me. And if I find out they did and you didn't let me know, you're gone as well. Now, fix it."

"Coach—" I begged.

"Don't try me," he cut me off, his voice ice. "There are Patinas and Krystals all over the place, begging to be in your spot. Praying to form the bond that y'all are so determined to break. Fix it."

Coach went back to the boys, who were practicing their blind handoff, leaving me and Krystal standing there, holding the metal stick, trying our best to not let our hands touch, which was pretty much impossible. Deja and Brit-Brat stood in front of us, awkward.

"Come on y'all, just squash it so we can get back to work," Brit-Brat said. "We a team."

"I ain't start it. She came for me for no reason," I pleaded my case.

"That's because you were purposely trying to make me look bad," Krystal said.

"Make you look bad? I was running. Running. This is a track team."

"Yo, you think I don't know that? I was on this team before you!"

"That's the thing. You don't think I know that!" Krystal didn't say nothing back. She just looked at me with a screwface, then yanked the baton. I almost let go.

"Whoa, whoa! Chill," Deja said, eyes wide, hands up.

"Yeah, y'all trippin'. Let's just talk it out," Brit-Brat said. "I've watched enough Iyanla Vanzant to know how to do this."

"When do you have time to watch Iyanla Vanzant?" Deja asked. "I didn't even know she still had a show."

"I don't think she do, but my mother recorded every single episode and uses it whenever she feels like she don't understand me. I keep trying to tell her, I'm tall and skinny with big feet, and therefore a monster. And then she says, no baby, you're beautiful, and I'm here for you, and what do you need from me to support you—which she steals from Iyanla—and then I say, a bag of Twizzlers, a trip to the mall, and a lock on my door, and then she says, how about a bag of Twizzlers, and then I say I hate everyone and everything."

"Wait, so you don't get the Twizzlers?" Deja asked, now laughing.

"What? Oh, of course I get the Twizzlers."

"I love Twizzlers," Krystal said, low. It was as if suddenly we were all just thinking about candy.

"Me too. My mother used to sell them," I said after an uncertain pause. I wasn't sure if I wanted to join in on this weird Twiz-fest that had suddenly broken out. Especially since I was just about to give Krystal a good old-fashioned Beverly Jones Funky Zone beat-down. But it seemed like it was happening, so . . .

"Your mother?" This from Krystal.

"Yeah, she used to be the candy lady in Barnaby Terrace."

"Wait, that white lady sold candy in Barnaby Terrace?" she asked.

"That's not my mother. That's my auntie."

Krystal was quiet. For once. Probably trying to swallow down all that "loud-and-wrong" she'd just spat.

Brit-Brat stepped in. "Okay, so what Iyanla would say, now that we've broken the ice, is, 'Patty, what did Krystal say to offend you?'" Then she changed her mind. "You know what, scratch that question. I think we know what you both said. Yeesh. How about this. Patty, what's one thing you want Krystal to know about you?"

Brit-Brat had her hands clasped and was leaning in like she really knew what she was doing. Like she was for real. I couldn't believe I was actually about to do this, but seeing how serious Brit was, I felt like I had to.

"I wasn't trying to embarrass her."

"Say it to her, not to me," Brit-Brat nudged, her voice over-the-top calm. *Seriously?*

"I wasn't trying to embarrass you," I said, feeling totally ridiculous. But also feeling like Krystal needed to know that, because it was true. "And I'm sorry for not adjusting like we learned when we were doing the waltz. But I'm still figuring everything out."

"Yes. Yes, we all are. We're trying to figure out this relay race . . . of life," Brit-Brat said, her eyes now shut. Now we all shot looks at her, like really? And when she opened hers and realized we were staring her down, she said, "What? That's what Iyanla would say." She turned to Krystal. "Your turn."

Krystal sighed. "Look, even though I talk a lot of trash, I'm serious about this team too," she assured me. "But . . . it's real that I'm . . . I'm not as fast as you."

jason reynolds

"Shoot, neither am I," Brit-Brat seconded. "But that don't mean we can't win if we stay connected."

"Exactly," Deja chimed.

I looked at Krystal. She looked at me. But for the first time today, neither of us were sizing each other up. You know how you can tell if a person is looking at you, or *looking* at you? Yeah, there was none of that extra sting in her eyes. She was just . . . looking at me. Like she was trying to see me.

"We good?" I asked, still holding on to the stupid baton. Krystal bit down on her bottom lip, nodded.

"Yeah, we good."

"Good, because I'm done with Iyanla Van-CANT over here." Deja smirked.

Brit-Brat palmed both of Deja's shoulders and looked in her eyes all serious. "Oh, please. You know you want me to fix your life." Deja rolled her eyes, like tuh. "Okay. But just know, denial is the first step to defeat, Deja."

A few minutes later we called Whit over. We would've called Coach, but he was so mad at us that it just didn't seem like a good idea.

"Can we drop the baton?" I asked.

"Can you what?" Whit sparked up like I had asked

112

her for twenty bucks. "You can never, ever drop the baton."

"That's not what I meant."

"But it is. Subconsciously." Everybody was Iyanla all of a sudden. "But if y'all are done fighting, you can release it. Krystal, you keep it, and we can get back to practice."

"We're straight," I said.

"You sure?"

I looked at Krystal. Saw her. Saw all of us, and knew we now had each other's backs. "Yeah, Whit. We good."

TO DO: Think about aliens and rap music
(and Dad)

"HOW WAS PRACTICE?" Momly asked as usual, turning the radio down as I closed the car door.

"Fine," I said, right on script, as Momly drove away from MLK Park. Even though I felt like I looked normal, apparently I didn't.

"What's wrong?" she asked.

Maddy, who had been kicking the back of my seat, suddenly stopped. Listened closely for my answer.

"Nothing. Why?" The only thing I could guess was that even though all the drama at practice was over, some of it must've been lingering in me. On me. You know how you clear your throat? How you force an almost-cough to get the crackly stuff out? Well, I tried to clear my face. Tried to open my eyes wider and loosen my jaw a little to wipe it back to regular.

"You just seem off, that's all."

"Nah, I'm cool," I insisted, then changed the subject. "Maddy, you need me to help you with your homework?"

"No. We already did it. Momly helped me," she said, then started kicking the seat again.

Momly turned the radio up. No music. Just talk. People talking about people talking about animals like they people. Which Momly thought was hilarious, Maddy thought it was fascinating because of her upcoming field trip to the farm, and I thought was bang-your-head boring.

"My mother used to take her dog to the spa. Like, the spa . . . for humans. Used to get the ugly mutt massages and facials as if her Chihuahua was living some kind of stressful life. It was unbelievable. That money could've gone to her grandchildren for college, for goodness' sake. But since the dog couldn't get a degree, it was like she didn't care. I mean, can you imagine?" a lady on the radio went on and on. *Yes, I can imagine,* I thought, T-N-T and

Becca instantly replacing the Krystal track drama in my head (and apparently on my face), reminding me to tell Momly about my group project "after-school meet-up" thingy I had to do the next day. I bet Becca had one of those little dogs. Probably dressed it up like her twin. Oh boy.

"Hey, so tomorrow after practice, can you take me back over by the school to this girl in my class's house?" I asked. "It's for the Frida project."

"After practice?" Momly turned the radio down again. "Will her parents be there?"

"Her grandmother," I explained.

Momly nodded. "And who is this young lady?"

"Her name is Becca Broward. She's okay. I mean, I just want to get it over with so I can get a good number on this project, y'know, to keep Ma off my back." And not to mention, my feet on the track. Momly could definitely understand that.

"Okay." There was some hesitation in her voice. "Well, you want me to bring you a change of clothes?" I hadn't even thought about that. The last thing I needed was to show up at Becca's house smelling like sweat gravy. Before I could even answer, Momly added, "I'll just pack a little bag for you."

➤

At home, after homework, turkey wings, and push-ups with Maddy, Maddy and me laid around in her room, looking at old-school music videos on my laptop while I counted the beads left on her braids. I know the nineties videos seem a little weird, but me and Cotton always watched them, let them play one after another. And because we'd been doing it for so long, Maddy liked them too. Knew all the songs and everything. We loved Mary J. Blige, and that came from my mom. She really got on a Mary kick after my father passed and played her nonstop when we were little. It was truly all about Jesus and Mary. And I get it. I mean, just the way Mary be dancing is worth watching, like she a sixty-year-old man who just hit the lottery. Like she got all dressed up in a fur vest and knee boots, full face of makeup and hair fresh-laid, just to go beat somebody up. To go fight life. Like she had all the answers to all the questions.

And I needed some of them answers. Not just for the track, but also for school—and after school—the next day. Answers for Mr. Winston as he went on and on shouting, "'Cannon to right of them! Cannon to left of them!' Are ye part of the six hundred? Are ye part of the Light Brigade?" Answers for Ms. Teller in math class as she asked us to describe a cylinder. And even worse, when she asked us to describe a trapezoid, which I wanted to raise my hand and say, "A trapezoid is another name for a scary kidnapper." But instead I decided to save that joke for me and Cotton.

I also needed an answer to the cafeteria, which to me, always asked the same question, "Where you sitting?" I didn't just assume I was gonna have another spot over at Becca's table. So instead of me going in there thinking that, and playing myself, I just did my usual. Got my food, which today was short rib, which was delicious and a little weird because I couldn't help but think about what animal has a rib this short. I know they say it's beef, but don't no cow have a little baby rib like this. And then I started thinking about the radio, about the people talking about people who talk about animals like they people, and I just . . . I just . . . lost my appetite.

For like five minutes.

For one lap around the cafeteria.

Then Becca called me over again. And I (almost did my Mary J. Blige walk over there and) sat down and separated the meat from the bone, while Becca, for the second day in a row, went on about music . . . in space.

"Seriously, my father said there's like all kinds of

stuff on this gold record they sent up there back in the seventies. And not just music. But he said there's digital photos of people eating and dancing and stuff."

"So you're saying, somewhere up in the stars, there's just random information about us floating around?" the girl sitting next to her, the girl I still didn't know but that I heard Becca call Sasha, asked. She said it in that I-don't-believe-you voice, and I couldn't blame her. Becca was buggin'.

"Yep. But it's on a gold record. They did it thinking that maybe one day aliens would find it and learn about us."

Today Macy Franks was sitting directly across from me. She dragged hunks of meat across her plate, sopping up sauce before lifting her fork to her mouth. She chewed, swallowed, then pointed her fork at Becca and asked, "But if aliens do find it, won't they need a record player to play it on?"

"We don't even really use those things down here anymore!" Sasha said.

"Plus, what makes you think aliens don't already know about us? Shoot, I know a few aliens in this school," Macy added.

The other girls laughed.

"Oh yeah? Like who?" Becca asked.

I looked down at my plate. Chewed my lip for a second like it was a piece of beef.

"Like me," Macy replied, shaking her head. "And obviously, you!"

Phew. Shoulders back, Patina.

The conversation went on, Becca leading the way, now asking everybody if they could record anything on whatever gold record she was talking about, what would it be.

"I mean, choose carefully, because it's gonna last forever and might be seen or heard by aliens," she reminded us.

"I wish I could send what my older brother's shoes smell like," Sasha said. "I feel like aliens won't want anything to do with us, not attack us or anything, if they knew what kinds of smells come out of teenage boys." I chuckled at that one, only because I spend so much time around boys, I can definitely cosign. It's like their toes be made of week-old cheesy bread or something.

"This is true," Macy said, now folding her meat-less plate. "I'd probably send some origami. Maybe a fortune-teller with instructions on how to use it. And under every flap it would say, Come to earth, destroy Chester Academy, located at . . . What's the address here? Whatever . . . destroy the school, find your sisters Macy and Becca, and take them home."

"Speak for yourself!" Becca's voice rang an octave higher than normal, putting her at almost glass-shatter level. "Anyway, what about you, Patina? And don't say anything about Frida Kahlo, either. That's cheating."

I could've used some short rib to stuff into my face to keep me from having to say anything. The seat was enough, and to be honest, I wasn't really expecting any actual words to come my way. So I wasn't ready. Caught off guard. But everyone was looking at me, waiting for an answer. I ran through—and this is gonna sound silly—everything I would want an alien to know about me. About Barnaby Terrace, and my folks. Where I'm from. But I couldn't really figure out what I would want to go up into space. Pictures? Movies? Red beads? All my first-place ribbons? Better yet, get rid of my stupid second-place one?

"Um . . . it could be anything?" I stalled.

"Yep. I mean, when they first did it, they sent a bunch of music recordings and stuff."

"They send rap music?" I asked.

"Good question," Macy propped.

Becca looked stumped. She tapped her temple. "Hmmm. I don't . . . I don't think so."

"Probably not," I agreed, "because it wasn't really a thing at the time. So . . ." And then it hit me. Something I never really thought about. Something I never even really heard. But it was important to my family in a weird way. Important to me in a way that kinda lived in the part of my brain that I can't even think with. It's like an under-thought or something like that. Hard to explain. "Back in the day, my father used to make beats. I think I'd try to send one of those up there. Either that, or maybe his favorite cupcake recipe." I sorta shrugged. "I know, super random."

"I want some cupcakes right now," a girl whose hair was spun into a tight bun the size of a biscuit on the tip-top of her head said. I hadn't caught her name yet. I don't think anybody said it.

"Cupcakes would be cool," Sasha agreed. But Becca's mind was somewhere else.

"Yeah, they would be, but what would really be cool is beats, right? I mean, especially if some alien DJ got ahold of them." Becca did a fake DJ thing with her hand on her plate, like she was scratching records. And then she added, "Does your dad still make beats?" But her voice seemed to slow down, stretched out and distorted all crazy in my ears.

D o e S Y O u R d A D S t i L L m a K E B e A t s ?

My throat. Did I eat the plate without knowing? Did the pointy fingers of the fork break off? Did I swallow them, so now plastic nails were poking the inside of my neck? I never, ever, ever talked about my father in public. Not because I didn't want to, but because it just never came up. I was more used to talking about my mother. My mothers. The mom situation always became a conversation about why I have two, but never about why I don't have a dad. If anything, most people just assume Uncle Tony's my pops, which is cool, but it just never hit me that I don't really talk about my actual dad. Not even to Cotton. Not to nobody. And so this simple question about whether or not my dad still makes beats tightened the skin around my bones.

"Patina?" Becca's voice wah-wah'd in my head. "You okay? You look sick." I had no idea how long I was sitting there, stuck.

"No . . . um, sorry," I tried to answer. "My father . . . yeah, he, um . . . he's . . ."

Gone.

But before I could actually say it, the bell rang and it was off to history class, where I had to sit with it all. Had to let the thought of my dad splash around my stomach with whatever a short rib was, while my regular-size ribs felt like they were being bent. A tiny hammer, the one that always knocks on the back of my throat whenever I need to cry, knocking away! And usually, whenever I feel this stuff, it's soothed by the thought of track practice. By running. But since it was now thundering out—causing Becca to almost jump out of her skin every five minutes in Ms. Lanford's class, which, along with me struggling to get myself together, kept "Group Frida" from getting any work done—Coach sent out a text saying practice was canceled. The world was proving it hated me. It was like the ultimate hair flip. Like the Earth's ha-ha-ha.

TO DO: Think about aliens in big fancy houses (and posers)

NOT ONLY DOES rain mean no practice, but rain on Wednesday means Thursday's practice—the last practice before the meet on Saturday—was gonna suck. Too bad to even think about. And I had no time to think about it anyway, because no practice also meant I didn't have an excuse not to go straight to Becca's after school.

I met Maddy in the north wing, walked her to the car as usual. Well, it was more like a run to the car, because the rain was coming down hard. Maddy climbed in and I jumped in the passenger seat.

"Practice is canceled," I blurted at Momly, wiping water from my arms.

"I figured," she replied, smirking. I kicked something on the floor. A plastic bag. Fresh clothes and stuff that she'd packed for me anyway. Just in case.

"So, if it's okay with you, I think I'm just gonna go over the girl, Becca's, house to work on the group project now. That way I don't have to stay long." Momly didn't say nothing to that, just nodded. "Can you please, please, please come get me in two hours."

"Two hours, got it," she confirmed. "But do you know where she lives?" I just pointed from the window. The big house directly across the street. Momly looked, let her mouth hang open for a second before catching herself. "Wow. Um . . . well, I guess I'll just drive you on over there."

And just then Becca, Taylor, and TeeTee appeared in the doorway of the school, but because of the rain, they didn't come out. And if they were planning to wait the storm out, they would never get to Becca's house, which meant there was no reason for me to go. Plus, we'd never get any work done.

"There go the other girls in my group right there," I said, the words like glue on my tongue, only because I knew what Momly would say next. But, like I said, it was raining. Hard. And we all had to get to the same place.

"Oh, well then, I'll just take all of you!"

Momly beeped the horn and waved Becca, Taylor, and TeeTee over. They didn't come. Not at first. Momly's sweet face can definitely come across as stranger-danger if you don't know her. But then she cracked the window enough to be heard and shouted, "I'm Patina's auntie!" and the girls came running to the car.

Maddy got up front with me, something that Momly would never, ever allow any other time, but it was only, and I do mean only, because we were going right across the street that Momly let it slide. Didn't matter to Maddy. She was in the front seat, and she was happy. Smashed in the back was basically my worst nightmare. I'm kidding. But seriously, it was wild to know that Becca, Taylor, and TeeTee were crammed into Momly's car, which is basically like my car!

"Seat belts, everyone," Momly sang. I yanked the seat belt around Maddy and me, strapping her tight to my chest. I couldn't even turn around to look at Becca and them. Not because the seat belt was too tight, but because it was all just too weird. I wasn't embarrassed or nothing. I take that back. I was a little embarrassed, only because Momly was playing her talk radio, and

Maddy decided to try out some small talk by asking if any of them gave their dogs massages or kissed them on their mouths.

"Maddy," I snapped as she turned halfway around to get a good look at the girls.

"What? I'm just askin'."

"I don't have a dog," Becca said, cheery.

"Neither do we," TeeTee said for her and Taylor.

"Well, y'all got mothers?" Maddy followed up.

"Oh, that's enough, Madison," Momly tsked, putting an arm across both me and Maddy as she came to a red light.

"I'm just asking," Maddy repeated.

"Of course we all have moms. Why?" Taylor asked, which stung me a little. Because we all don't have everything. Some people have mothers, some don't. Some have dads, some don't. Some got two moms. Shoot, some even have to be moms before they actually are moms. The light changed and Momly rolled across the street so slowly that cars were honking their horns and zooming around us.

"Oh, okay. I just thought maybe you didn't because you got all that makeup on, and my mother says that if—"

"Okay, I think we're almost there, right, Becca?" I

cut Maddy off before she got me cut off. Even more cut off.

Becca laughed. T-N-T, not so much.

"Yep, this is me right here on the left. The one with the open gate." Becca pointed to the most giant-est house I ever seen up close. Momly pulled in, pulled up around this big fountain, to the front door.

As everybody got out, I leaned back in and reminded Momly, "Two hours. Please. Just two hours."

"Two hours," she repeated slowly, putting two fingers up. And Maddy, who had now climbed back in the backseat, also put two fingers up, but held them up to the window at Becca and the girls—a peace sign.

INSIDE BECCA'S HOUSE:
(1) A whole lot of space.
(2) A big piano Becca called "that old piece
     of crap."
(3) A chandelier that looked like the ceiling
     was raining diamonds.
(4) Paintings. Pictures of paintings.
     Paintings of pictures. And pictures. Of
     Becca. Looking goofy.
(5) A movie theater that Becca said no one
     ever used.

(6) Big furniture made from the same kind
   of leather as my uncle's favorite jacket.

(7) No dog.

(8) A scraggly cat named Carl, that didn't
   wear clothes or look like it had ever
   had a massage a day in its life.

(9) Me and the two other girls, who were
   taking selfies like they ain't never been
   nowhere.

(10) The familiar smell of sugar.

"This is Granny," Becca said as we popped into the kitchen for a moment. An old lady dressed like an old lady was baking cookies.

"Hi, girls," she said, scooping batter from a bowl. "Sweets will be ready in a short while." The old lady's voice was like Momly's if it had a whole bunch of cuts in it.

"We're going to be upstairs doing work, Granny."

"Okay, well then, I won't bother you. They'll be down here. Chocolate chip, oatmeal, snickerdoodle, and peanut butter. You girls help yourselves."

"She made all that?" I asked.

"Yeah, it's her hobby. We don't even eat them. She just likes to make them and then give them away to our neighbors. I like cupcakes better. What's your dad's favorite recipe?"

I don't know if it was the sugar smell, or the buildup from earlier, or what, but I just . . . said it.

"He passed away."

Becca looked me in the eye. Straight in the eye. "I'm . . . I'm sorry. I didn't know."

"It was a long time ago." And now, relieved I got it over with, I changed the subject without actually changing the subject. Another one of those small-talk tips I picked up from Momly. "Where your folks?" I really asked because the house was so quiet. No TV. No radio. No noise besides pans being slid into the oven, and the weird giggles of T-N-T holding their cell phones in the air, posing.

"Where they always are. At work," Becca shot back. "Come on." And with Taylor and TeeTee trying for the millionth time to get the whole chandelier in the shot, I followed behind Becca as we walked up one of those round-and-round stairs to her room.

Here's the thing about hair-flipper bedrooms, they basically only come one way. I mean, I had never actually been in one in real life, but I had seen them enough times on TV to know that they're all bedazzled in pink and purple. They look like candy shops. Like

jason reynolds

doll houses. Like living inside of a strawberry cupcake.

But as we entered Becca's room . . . uhhhhh . . . blackness. Not like Black History Month blackness. And not blackness like I passed out from the overload of girlyness in Becca's room. I didn't. Though I did feel like I was gonna black out from shock, because if Becca's house was a castle, Becca's room in this house was the dungeon. The upstairs dungeon. Everything . . . eh-ver-ree-thing in her room was black. The walls, the closet doors, the lamps and lights, the desk, the ceiling, everything. It was like Becca was really a YMBC or something. Like she was really a button-bagger!

As I tried to hide my shock, Taylor and TeeTee finally came busting in the room all squeals and smiles, which quickly turned into gasps and frowns. Their faces were stuck, half-melted. Terrified. Meanwhile, Becca pulled a chair from behind her door, another from the desk against the wall, and plopped down on her bed like none of this was a big deal.

"Okay. Let's get to work on Miss Frida." She clapped her hands together, excited.

Silence. From me and T-N-T, whose struggle-faces looked like they were trying to swallow their own tongues. Me, well, all I kept telling myself was, two hours. Just two hours, Patty.

"Yeah, let's get to . . . work," I finally said, and before I could grab one of the chairs, TeeTee and Taylor had already snatched them, positioned them right next to each other, and right next to the door. So I sat on the bed. Take it easy. No big deal. All-black room . . . no problem. No problem at all. Don't really mean nothing. Nope. Not at all. Not. At. All.

Funny thing is, the group work went exactly the same as it did in school. Me, basically trying to manage it all while T-N-T, who were usually distracted by paint on their nails, were now distracted by paint on the walls. So while me and Becca were digging around on the Internet for more details about our Mexican artist friend, Taylor and TeeTee were whispering to each other, until finally Becca said, "Are y'all gonna help?"

"Oh, yeah," Taylor said, shocked that she got called out.

"We just had a question about it all," TeeTee added. I don't know what Becca thought was coming next, but I thought it was going to be about Frida. Turns out, the "it all" they had a question about had nothing to do with the project. "What's the deal with . . . um . . . all this?" TeeTee waved her hands around like she was swatting flies.

"What do you mean?" Becca asked, in that honest way she was always asking something.

"I mean, this." TeeTee repeated the wave.

"Look, I'm not trying to be mean, but it's just . . . a little weird," Taylor jumped back in. "It's like at school, you act one way, and it's not all . . . um . . . goth-y like this, but really you . . ."

"She's what?" I asked, cocking my head to the side. I don't know where it came from, but something about the way they were talking rubbed me wrong. The same way I felt when people tried to mess with Ghost. Or Sunny. Or even Lu. But Becca didn't need me.

"Goth-y?" She was for-real confused. "Oh. You wanna know about the black." She smiled, totally unfazed. Becca reached behind her back and snatched the curtains closed. Then she got up and slapped the light switch on the wall. And then blackness went to darkness . . . and the whole universe appeared.

Stars and planets and whatever other things be up there in space popped out of the black, glowing green, all around us.

"What . . . is all this?" I asked, looking up at the ceiling.

"This is as much of the galaxy as you can fit in a bedroom. And that"—she leaned over to see what was directly above my head—"well, that looks like the Gemini Twins." She tried to get me to see what she was talking about, but it all just looked like a bunch of stars to me. "Constellations. Like connect the dots, except with stars, you know?" I didn't know. But I still thought it was kinda cool.

"I ain't never seen all these stars up there. I mean, I seen a few, but not like this."

"They're all up there. Each one connected to another in some weird way. It's amazing."

"Wild," I corrected her.

"Not that wild," she corrected my correction. "At least not to me. My folks are rocket scientists. This is pretty much as normal as it gets in this house."

"Rocket scientists?" Taylor finally found her words again.

"Well, they're really called astronautical engineers, basically the same thing."

"That's a real job?" TeeTee came right behind her. I can't front, I was thinking the exact same thing.

"I hope so. If not, I don't know where my parents are all the time." Becca laughed, but only a little. There was something about her face in that moment that was weird, like something invisible was pinching her underarm. I knew that face. Saw it in Ghost. And some people say they saw it in me. Shoot, it was probably the face I made at lunch. The might-be-sick face.

So I pointed at a cluster to my left. Becca hopped up. "Oh, that looks like Pegasus." And that did it. No more Frida. Becca was off, spazzing around her room, point- ing out different star clusters and planets, explaining why we can't see all of them where we live, straight up nerding out, and I was into it. But I guess T-N-T . . . not so much. They were basically just sitting there texting, and I figured they were texting each other talking trash about it all, but when Taylor blurted, "My mother's here," I realized who they were really texting.

"Already?" Becca asked, still not tripping about the way the girls had treated her. It was like nothing really bothered her, which I admired. "But you didn't even have any cookies."

"No, um, no . . . that's okay," TeeTee said, as if the cookies were going to be black too. Honestly, I was so caught up in her room that I'd forgotten all about the cookies.

"Yeah, it's cool. We just . . . have to go. Sorry," Taylor said, not seeming sorry at all.

"Well, let me walk you down," Becca insisted.

I checked the time and knew that the two-hour mark was coming, and one thing about Momly was she was never late. She was the most on-time person in the world. So it made sense for me to head downstairs too. And halfway down the fancy round-and-round steps with the crystal chandelier hanging over us like ice frozen in the air, my phone buzzed. It was Momly. She was here.

Becca opened the door, and Maddy was outside talking to someone.

"Mrs. S, what are you doing here?" Maddy squealed, as me, Becca, Taylor, and TeeTee came through the door. Maddy was standing at the passenger-side window of the other car in the driveway. The one that came for T-N-T. At least I thought it had come for T-N-T, but why would Maddy's teacher be here for them?

"I'm here to pick up my daughter, Taylor." What? Daughter? Taylor? "And this is my sister, Mrs. Dorsey. She teaches at the school too. Fourth grade."

"Hi, Madison. I've heard so much about you. Hopefully, you'll be in my class in a few years." Wait a minute. Taylor Stein. TeeTee Dorsey. Bestie-cousin-sisters. And daughters of . . . no way . . . teachers? Teachers. Tuh. Well, well, well. T-N-T. Regular girls.

I looked at the queen hair flippers, but guess what? They wouldn't look at me. Just shot off the step and trotted over to the car. And that's when I knew they knew they were caught. Gotcha! I could tell they knew what I was thinking. They knew I knew they'd been fronting this whole time. Ain't no teachers rich, and I knew that because at Barnaby, they told us all the time. *They don't pay me enough to teach you and babysit you.* Now I got why T-N-T were acting all weird in Becca's house. Taking selfies at the piano and all that. Chandelier shots for days. I turned back to Becca. It was like she hadn't even noticed. She just waved at them, while at the same time Maddy waved me over.

"Patty, it's my teacher, Mrs. S!" she said as I walked toward the car.

"I see! Hi, Mrs. S." I tried to keep my cool. "Happy early birthday. Taylor says y'all got plans tomorrow. Hope you have a great time!"

And before I got in the car, I looked up at the sky. Still cloudy. But I looked for stars anyway. Of course, I didn't see none. But now, for some reason, it felt good just knowing there were more up there than I'd ever known.

TO DO: Be introduced to Momly
(like, for real)

I HAD NEVER talked so much at dinner, but I was going on about Becca's house, how beautiful it all was, and how Becca's room was nothing like I expected.

"Stars everywhere. It was like being at the science center or something," I explained. "And did y'all know rocket scientists were real?"

Momly laughed and Uncle Tony joked me, talking about, "It don't take a rocket scientist to know rocket scientists are real, Patty." I admit, he got me.

I tried to explain to Maddy what constellations were, telling her they were stars connected in the sky

139

to make pictures. She said her teacher told them about constellations before, which of course made me go in on her teacher's daughter. Bony McPhony and her cousin, Lie-Lie. All this time I'd been thinking about Taylor and TeeTee like they were some kind of royalty, when really they were just . . . regular girls pretending to be something they not. Cornballs.

"But you don't know, maybe they have fathers that are doing well?" Momly suggested, her voice tired.

"Come on, babe," Uncle Tony cut in. "If I hit it big, you think you'd decide to be around all them snotty noses—matter fact, snotty, snotty noses—every day?" Then he quickly added, "Not you, Maddy. And I'm not trying to be mean, but . . . come on, y'all know what I'm sayin'."

"Well, how exactly do you plan on hitting it big?" Momly threw one of her zings that sound too sweet to be a zing, which makes it zingier.

"Oop!" I yelped, just to get Uncle Tony back for the rocket scientist burn.

"And also," Momly added, "Tony, you know me better than that. There's nothing I love more than a snotty nose. Snotty or not."

After dinner, I wanted to help Momly with the dishes, sensing how tired she was. Uncle Tony had cleared the table and was now helping Maddy get ready for bed. She was probably talking his ear off about going to the farm in the morning. I couldn't wait to hear what she thought of it, only because I remember when I went—every school in the city goes to the same one. Maybe it's because they got so many cows, and that's cool, but milking cows might've been the grossest thing I've ever done. I mean . . . yeah. It's up there.

I ran the water in the sink.

"Oh, don't worry about the dishes, Patty. I'll take care of them in a minute," Momly said, now bending down, sweeping nothing into a dustpan.

"I got it."

"No, it's okay," she insisted. But I was already squirting green liquid soap on everything.

"Seriously, it's fine. I can do it."

Momly didn't say nothing to that. Just emptied the dustpan in the trash, then put the broom back in the kitchen closet. She snatched a hand towel from the oven handle.

"Then I'll dry."

I scrubbed each plate, then handed it over to Momly, who wiped it, then put it back up in the cabinet. We did this over and over again with dishes and silverware, until there was nothing left but cups.

"I just can't believe those girls," I went on, handing Momly a glass. Just couldn't get over it.

"I can." She set the glass down. "I knew a lot of girls like that. Shoot, I was almost one of them."

I ran water in the last glass, then turned the faucet off. "What you mean?" I asked, handing her the final cup.

"I mean, I remember when I first went to that school. To Chester." She dried the glass and set it on the counter. Then she folded the towel into a square, placed it on the counter as well.

"Wait. You went there?"

Momly smirked. "Yeah, a long time ago. I told you that." Had she? I didn't remember ever talking to her about going to Chester. Actually, if I'm being honest, I don't really remember talking to Momly about anything. At least not about her. Didn't realize that until that moment.

"I mean, maybe you did, but I don't remember."

"Uh-huh. Well, in case you missed it . . . I grew up in the country. Not too far from the farm I have to drive Maddy to tomorrow morning. And when I was ten, my parents split up, and my father pretty much

disappeared. My mother had to figure out how to support us, now that we were on our own, so she ended
up applying to be the custodian of Chester Academy.
And because she was an employee, I got to go there
for free."

I had no idea. I mean, about any of it. I didn't know
Momly went to Chester. I also didn't know her mom
was a janitor.

"Did you like it there?"

"Ha!" she yelped, then continued, "No. No, no, no.
Shoot, the only reason we sent you and Maddy there
is because I know the education is excellent. But, for
me, I couldn't stand it. Not at first. I mean, listen, I'm
a poor girl from the sticks who ended up in a fancy
city school. And what made it worse was after classes,
I couldn't just go home like everybody else. I had to
hang around with my mother, help her clean floors
and bleach toilets. Of course, eventually my classmates
found out, and then the jokes started. They called me
names like Emily Mop Bucket, stuff like that. A few of
the girls would even purposely leave trash around, or
spit their gum out on the floor, because they knew after
school my mother and I would have to clean it up."

"Stupid hair flippers." I murmured, chewing on the
words.

"What?"

"Nothing. Just . . . did it . . . like, did it ever get better?"

"Better?" Momly humphed. "Eventually. I mean, first I tried to fit in. Tried to find another poor kid to pick on to take the attention off me. But all the kids I went to tease ended up becoming my friends. And after that, school got better for a while. But there were other things that happened that made it tough again."

Uh-oh. "Other things like what?" I asked. Momly crossed her arms.

"Well, halfway through my seventh-grade year, my mother had a massive stroke. The whole left side of her body was basically paralyzed. So she couldn't do the job anymore. Luckily, my grades were good, and they pitied me, so the school let me stay through the eighth grade for free. But . . . that was hard. And I . . ." Momly drew in a breath, then continued. "And I, um, I didn't know how to deal with it, so I decided I would just keep doing her job, which I couldn't do because I was twelve years old, so obviously the school couldn't let me be the custodian, plus they had no idea I was helping my mother in the first place. So they ended up bringing on somebody else. A man named . . . Mr. Warren." She paused, giving me a second to catch on.

"You mean, *Mr. Warren*, Mr. Warren?" Mr. Warren, her favorite patient?

"Yep. Mr. Warren, Mr. Warren." I had never seen Mr. Warren, but in this moment, I wondered what he looked like back then. Probably real tall with big crusty hands, a rough beard, a beanie on his head or one of them old-men hats with the kangaroo on the back. Maybe even chewing on a straw or a toothpick, a fat wallet in his back pocket, full of receipts and no money. Something like that. Like Coach, if Coach had hair on his face and was a janitor. And was tall. So . . . maybe not like Coach. But . . . yeah.

"Mr. Warren's been the sweetest old man alive since back then," Momly continued. "He'd let me show up for work with him after school, and he'd say I could sweep here, or scrub there. Light work compared to what my mother had me doing, but it was all I needed to make me feel like I was honoring her, y'know, and like I wasn't completely taking a handout."

I nodded. All of this made perfect sense to me. "But where was your mom?"

"We had to put her in a home. I went to live with an older cousin who'd moved to the city for college. She was really too young to be taking care of me, but we didn't have any other family, so . . ." Momly shrugged.

"Yeah."

"But I saw my mom on weekends." Momly picked at a cuticle, gave it a tear. "Then one day I showed up after school ready for my daily task, and Mr. Warren said that he didn't have anything for me. And when I asked him why not, he said because he didn't have a task nearly as important as the one I was avoiding. Wait . . . that's not exactly what he said. What he really said was"—Momly held her finger out and screwed her face to imitate an old man—"'Folks who try to do everything are usually avoiding one thing.'"

"And was he right?" I asked, folding my arms across my chest.

"Was he right?" Momly picked up the last two glasses from the counter, held them up to the light— no spots—then put them up in the cabinet. "He definitely was. But I didn't know it at the time. I mean, I was twelve, and couldn't figure out how to deal with the fact that my mother wasn't the same, y'know?"

"Yeah."

"And guess what? That old man is still teaching me stuff. Even the other day, when he was sort of out of it, going on about buffing the floor"—Momly's face brightened, laughter trapped behind her lips—"all I

could think was that he thinks he can do things that
he just . . . he just can't anymore. In his mind, he's
strong enough to push a buffer. But you know? If he
really wants to clean that floor, we can do it together.
And that's okay."

TO DO: Get there
(there's nothing else I can do)

THE NEXT MORNING Momly dropped me off, but only me. Maddy had spent the whole ride telling me how milking cows didn't scare her, and how if the milk don't come out like it's supposed to, she'll just pick the whole cow up and shake the milk out of it. Yep, farm day had finally arrived.

"Have fun," I said, climbing out of the car at the exact same moment Becca was walking between Momly's car and the car in front of us. We did a weird wave thing, and then I turned back to Maddy. "You getting up front?" I asked, not really serious, but Momly cut me off anyway.

"No, Patty, she is not," she said with an unusual snap. Momly ain't have no funk in her. No sit down. No finger point. No talk-through-teethness. None of that. But she didn't do the Maddy-in-the-front-seat thing. Maddy could kick the front seat all day, every day, could put a hole in it and everything, and Momly would be cool. But not this.

"Come on, Momly. Please? I did it yesterday," Maddy begged. Momly turned around in her seat, looked Maddy in the face.

"You're not old enough yet, sweetheart." That little bit of snap was gone and she was back to sweet Momly, even though she was still saying no.

"Patty!"

"What you want me to do?" I shrugged. "Look, you'll be up front soon enough, and then all you gon' do is wish you were in the back. So chill, and enjoy your limo ride to the farm, Waffle." I tried not to laugh while closing the door and throwing up the peace sign.

This is gonna sound silly, but when I walked into school, the hallway seemed different. Just knowing that Momly used to clean the floors of Chester, used to make it shiny every day just so it could get all scuffed up and dirty again, the same way she did our house, her car, and everything else, had my mind doing flips,

jason reynolds

thinking thoughts it never thought before. I was looking down at the floor, the light shining off it. Looking down like usual, but for a different reason today.

At my locker, Becca was waiting for me, wearing a weirdo smile, holding a piece of paper.

"Hey," I said, surprised she was there.

"Hey. So, last night I was looking for more cool stuff about Frida, and I decided to just do something silly and Google Frida Kahlo and space, just to see, y'know? I wasn't really expecting nothing, but listen to this." Becca held the paper up and read, "'A constellation that exists only on paper is useless.'" She slapped the note down to her side. I gave her a blank stare. A *so what* face, which is when Becca yipped, "Frida said that!"

"But what does it mean?"

"I have no idea. But she said it!" Me and Becca laughed. "And I'm going to think about it, because maybe we can use it for the project."

I nodded, smiled. "Then I'll think about it too."

"Sweet. By the way, your little sister is the cutest." Then Becca held up two fingers like Maddy and said all corny and awkward, "Peace."

Peace. That's the opposite of what came knocking on the door at the very end of homeroom. Mrs. Stansfield had taken roll, and the morning announcements happened, which was usually about permission slips and the day's lunch menu. Sesame chicken—yes! One of my favorite things to eat. My stomach started growling as I heard those two words come crackling through the intercom. So excited. And then Jasmine Stanger made her own morning announcement, that she had to take her belly button ring out. She lifted her shirt. Her belly button had turned into an alien. And my stomach stopped growling.

After the announcements and before the bell rang, the intercom speaker came buzzing back on.

"Mrs. Stansfield?" Ms. Durden's voice came growling through. Ms. Durden worked at the front desk in the office. Had a face like a baby doll and a voice like a car engine.

"Yes?"

"Can you please send Patina Jones to the office? Her uncle's here to pick her up."

My uncle? To pick me up? Why? What? I jumped up, grabbed my bag, and headed for the door. As I walked down the hallway, I could see Uncle Tony pacing back and forth.

"Uncle Tony?"

When he turned toward me, his face looked like there was ice under his skin. "Patty!"

"What you doing here?"

My heart was pounding even before he said what he said. The thing you never want to hear. Something I'd heard before, and never wanted to hear again. "Something's happened."

Something's happened.

Something's happened?

The bell rang.

"What? What . . . happened?" I asked, already heading for the doors as my classmates poured into the hallway, homeroom over. My legs felt heavy and my body was doing what it does when I run, but I wasn't running. I was walking, but it didn't really feel like I was doing that, either. I was just . . . moving.

"I'll tell you in the car." Uncle Tony grabbed my hand, squeezed it as he led the way.

"Is it Ma? Is something wrong with Ma?" There was something about him holding my hand, something about that moment that made everything around me fade into streaks of yellows, browns, and pinks. The hallway muted in my head. I could only hear my uncle.

"We've gotta get to the hospital," he answered, steering me toward his SUV. He broke into a jog.

We have to go. We had to go. To the hospital. To the HOSPITAL.

Unmute. One second of teenage noise explosion before barreling through the double doors.

"The hospital?!" I cried out. "Uncle Tony, what's going on? What's wrong with Ma?" But he didn't respond until we were in his SUV. He jammed the key into the ignition and pulled away from the curb. And before I could ask again, he looked me square in the face.

"Your mother is fine," he confirmed finally. And I could breathe. But only one breath. Because then Uncle Tony said, "But Momly and Maddy were in an accident."

"What . . . wha . . . do . . . whattayoumean, Momly, and . . . and Maddy? What are you talking about?" It was hard to find words, because it was hard to find breath. My whole body felt like it had been emptied out. Like I ain't have bones or blood or nothing inside.

Uncle Tony repeated. "I don't know how else to say it, Patty. They . . . they were in a car accident."

Like I said—the opposite of peace. Well, not really because the opposite of peace is war, and I wasn't at war. But there were definitely cannons going off in my brain, just like Mr. Winston had been talking about. To the left and to the right. And all over. Cannons shooting exploding cannonballs of worry. Explosions of, *Is Maddy okay? Please let Maddy be okay. And Momly? Is she hurt?*

Is she . . . Boom. Boom. Boom. All Uncle Tony knew was he'd gotten a call from the hospital, not ten minutes ago. He was just leaving for work. That all they said was there was an accident. That he didn't know much more than that. He kept one hand on the wheel, and with the other he reached over and took mine again. Squeezed tighter this time, like trying to squeeze some *it's gonna be okay* in me. Trying to squeeze his own scared away the same way I do for Maddy sometimes. Oh, Maddy. No one was kicking the back of my seat. *Maddy. Maddy, please, just . . . Momly, please, please, just . . . be . . . just be . . . breathing.*

"Have you called my mom?" I asked as we pulled into the hospital.

"Not yet."

I immediately pulled out my phone, but Uncle Tony patted my hand down as he wheeled the SUV into a parking space.

"Let's, um . . . let's just wait until we see what's what, okay? Y'know, get a diagnosis." He turned the key, killed the engine.

My heart lurched at diagnosis. There's "die" in that word.

TO DO: Be there
(and stop Maddy from *going there*)

MOMLY WAS ALIVE. The nurse at the front desk told us she was banged up pretty bad, and had a mild concussion and a broken arm.

"And what about Maddy?" I asked before she'd even finished saying "broken arm." My heart had turned into a frog trying to jump out my throat. My brain thinking bad things only. *I'm sorry, but she didn't make it* . . . No. No, no, no. Don't think that. Don't think that. But I couldn't help it. What if Maddy was . . . I tried not to think what I couldn't stop myself from thinking. That Maddy, my mini-me, my Waffle, was . . . hurt. Was . . . gone. I tried to speak clear, my voice balling up like a piece of paper. "I mean, Madison. Madison Jones."

"The little girl who was with her," Uncle Tony made plain, his voice sharp. Almost too clear.

"Ah." The nurse's face brightened up. "Baby ain't have a scratch on her."

All the breath in my body left, and then came rushing back in. Filled me up with a bunch of thank goodness. The cannons stopped firing. And the *boom-boom-boom* became the *beep-beep-beep* coming though the crack in the door of the room Maddy and Momly were in. It was as if me and Uncle Tony had teleported there.

"Hello?" Uncle Tony cried out as he tapped on the door and crept in like we didn't belong there, like we were afraid the doctor who was also in the room would think we had come to steal our family back.

"Patty!" Maddy jumped up from a chair and crashed against me. She squeezed, not like she was trying to lift me up, but like she was trying to melt into me. And I squeezed back like I was scared to let go.

Uncle Tony darted to the bed where Momly lay. Maddy and me weren't far behind him. The first thing I noticed was Momly's face. It was puffed up, so much purple on her pale skin. Bruises and lumps and knots, worse than a Barnaby beat-down. And then I noticed her arm. The broken one. It was swollen up to the shoulder, making the skin look like it was being stretched too tight. Compared to the other arm, it looked more like a leg, at least the top part did. The bottom part they had in some kind of sling-contraption thingy, to keep it from moving. But I could still see the imprint in the fabric where the bone jutted out, like a second elbow. Looked like it hurt like crazy.

"Come on in, y'all." Momly's voice was all grog. She waved us toward her with her good arm—her right arm—like she was hosting a party. "Dr. Lancaster, this is the rest of my family. Patty, and my husband, Tony."

"Nice to meet you," Uncle Tony said, immediately shaking the doctor's hand.

"The pleasure's mine," Dr. Lancaster said, smooth. "Me and Maddy are just here making sure Mrs. Emily doesn't fall asleep while she's concussed."

"What happened?" I asked, because how does someone who drove as safe as Momly, someone who didn't even listen to music in her car, get in a crash?

"Yeah, Em, what in the world happened?" Uncle Tony followed up, gently stroking Momly's hair.

Momly's eyes were half-open, blinking super slow

like windshield wipers on the low setting. Like when it's just drizzling. "Someone ran a red light. Smacked right into us and kept going."

"A hit-and-run?" Uncle Tony asked, his voice hardening in a way I'd never heard.

Momly nodded. "Yeah." She tried to shift in the bed but was in too much pain to do so. Every little inch up or to the side made her show teeth. A pain smile. "But I'll be fine," she was telling us now, stroking Uncle Tony's arm. "Right, doc? Concussions and broken bones heal. I'm just glad the strongest girl in the world's not hurt."

Maddy's arm tightened around my waist. Down, tears. Down! Hold it together. You are Patina Jones. Daughter of Beverly Jones. No junk. No punk.

"I know," I said, forcing a small smile and resting my cheek on the top of Maddy's head. I figured I'd better put my face down somewhere before it split down the middle. Then Maddy reached over and took Momly's hand, her chest heaving as she worked to fight back her own feelings, even though she had been there the whole time. It was like now that me and Uncle Tony showed up, she could let herself be scared.

"It's okay, Maddy. I'm fine. I swear. It's just a broken arm. Remember when Cotton broke her arm? She was better in no time! Nothing crazy." Cotton broke her arm trying to prove she could do a handstand on the bathroom sink at Barnaby Elementary, but she slipped. She was lucky. Could've broke her neck. Or broke her life. But that would've been her own fault. This was different. "Hey . . . hey, Patty, I won't be running any relays anytime soon, huh? No handoffs for me." Momly was trying to lighten the mood, but it fell flat. I forced a fake laugh, because I got what she was trying to do. But jokes were Uncle Tony's thing.

"But . . . but . . . I just don't want them to anfiltrate it!" Maddy wasn't distracted at all by the corny comedy. Momly refocused.

"They're not gonna amputate it, baby. They're gonna fix it," she assured her. That voice, the one that usually only a mom has, even though . . . well, she's our mom too, kicked in and seemed to calm the whole room down. But I knew Maddy. I could look in her face and see that she wasn't so sure that things were going to be fine.

"Maddy, they're not gonna take it," I echoed. Then a better idea to chill Maddy out sprouted up in my mind, and I walked to the other side of the room to grab one of the two chairs that were there.

"We're definitely not," the doctor confirmed. And

while he explained how bone healing works, and Maddy started getting into how our mother had had her legs cut off, I bent down and pretended to try to move the chair. I started grunting like I was constipated or something, just to draw attention. "Ughn . . . ughn." I turned around and Maddy was still going on about how for our mom, first it was a toe, then it was a foot, then her legs—none of which she actually remembers—and how for Momly, what if it starts with one part of the arm, and the next thing you know half her body is cut off.

"What if she can't drive with half a body?" she asked the doctor, who at this point looked somewhere between amused and confused.

"Maddy, can you come help me, please?"

"Help you what?" she asked, her voice still quavering.

"Help me move this chair. It's too heavy." The chair really was more like real furniture. Not some flimsy fold-up. Of course I could've moved it if I really wanted to. But I bent down again with a huge, "Ughn!"

"It's just a chair, Patty," Maddy said, skeptical but coming to my side anyway.

"Yeah, but I think hospital chairs be heavier for some reason."

Maddy frowned, but then she grabbed the chair by the armrests and yanked it forward. I widened my eyes as Maddy backed the chair across the room, inch by inch, until it was at the foot of Momly's bed.

"That one's for Uncle Tony," I said as she slapped her hands together like, light work. "But I need to sit down too." I pointed at the other chair. "And then you can sit on my lap." Maddy trotted back to the other side of the room to get the other one, Uncle Tony plopping down in the first.

"Thank you, Maddy," he said, winking at Momly.

"No problem. They not even that heavy for me," Maddy boasted.

"Of course not," I agreed, watching her lug the next chair. When she'd parked it beside the other, I sat down. "Girl, I'm so glad we got somebody strong in this family." I patted my thighs, beckoning her to come take a seat so we could continue on with the visit and put the tears and scary stuff behind us. But, in true Maddy fashion, she wasn't ready to sit yet. Oh no. I got her going. Got her all revved up. Next thing I know she was now explaining to the doctor that she was one of the strongest first graders he'd ever seen.

"It's true," Momly gurgled.

And when Dr. Lancaster asked, "Is that right?"

Maddy ran up on him like a maniac, threw her arms around his legs, and tried to lift him!

"Wha . . . Whoa, whoa!" the doctor hooted.

"Maddy!" both Uncle Tony and Momly barked, clearly embarrassed. And me, well, I actually thought it was kind of awesome. I mean, think about it. Here we all are, sad about what happened to Momly—and what could've happened to Maddy—and somehow (thanks to me, ahem) we got from there to watching Maddy try to lift the doctor up off the floor.

"I . . . got it. I . . . can . . . do it!" she growled, yanking at the doctor's legs, his pants lifting enough to see his yellow dress socks. The doctor looked at me. I looked at him. He smiled, and then raised slowly up on his tiptoes just enough.

"What? How did you . . . ?" Dr. Lancaster gasped. Maddy let him go, stood back up, breathing heavy and nodding like some kind of warrior.

"I told you," she said to the doctor, then turned to the rest of us. "Told y'all."

"Lord have mercy," Momly muttered under her breath, shaking her head slightly. If only Ma had heard her, we would've had to go into a whole Sunday service right here in the hospital. "Okay, Maddy, that's enough. You've . . . proven your point."

But . . . she hadn't. It was like she had roid rage. That's what it's called when you take steroids and get all jacked and then start flipping out, right? Roid rage. It was like she had that. Because you wouldn't believe what she did next. She came back over to where me and Uncle Tony were sitting, and I thought she finally was going to hop up on my lap, but instead she turned toward Momly and grabbed the bed frame. "I can lift up this whole bed, with Momly in it!"

"NOOO!" everyone—everyone—shouted, and I sprang from my seat and grabbed Maddy before she could even try. Not that she would've really been able to lift it, but still, anything's possible, and then one broken arm is two broken arms and a broken back.

But thankfully, nothing, at least nothing like that, happened.

What did happen was Dr. Lancaster finally explained to Uncle Tony that Momly would have to have surgery to set and pin the bone.

"And when is this surgery?" Uncle Tony asked.

"Well, we wanted to do it today, but like I said, we have to monitor the concussion. So we'll need to do it tomorrow morning."

➤

We stayed at the hospital for a few more hours until finally Momly basically forced us to leave, saying we didn't have to go back to school but that I could not miss track practice. I was surprised. Maybe she knew that I wouldn't have been able to focus in class, probably resulting in me getting in trouble for finally letting one of them fake hair flippers have it. Or maybe she knew I needed practice. I needed to run.

And I did, even though, because yesterday's practice had been rained out, this would be the last practice before the meet on Saturday. I was fully prepared for the hardest practice ever.

TO DO: Run forever
(and then run some more)

WELL, NOT FULLY prepared.

Thursday. Long-run day. No surprise there. But because we were also training for relay races, Coach had to figure out how to combine both endurance and relay into the same workout. Which basically means, Coach had to figure out how to crush us.

"Patty, you okay?" Ghost whispered to me as we stretched—left-side toe touches. Aaron was counting down from ten.

"Yeah," I said. "Why?"

"Six, five, four . . . ," Aaron chanted.

"I'ono," Ghost said, now mid-yawn. Said he stayed up all night watching some movie about Jesse Owens, which was fine for him since he didn't have to go school. Spring break life. Ghost's tongue was a weird shade of purple, dyed from something. Candy, I guessed. "You just seem . . . different."

"Switch!" Aaron said. We all stretched to the right. With my eyes I followed my right arm, top part, elbow, bottom part, wrist, hand. All there. All working. I couldn't help but have a flash of Momly. And even though I knew she'd be okay—at least I hoped she'd be okay—it was hard to not wonder how everything was going to get done now. Would Uncle Tony have to drive us everywhere? Drop us off at school, pick us up? Then pick me up from track? What about dinner? What about Ma? Who was going to take care of Ma? And how was she going to go get her blood cleaned? I couldn't take her. I would if I could, but I can't drive! It was impossible to not think about all these things. These things that I hadn't really thought about because Momly always just . . . did them. Which I also never . . . really . . . thought about.

It was also impossible to just come to the track and pretend like I hadn't just come from the hospital. The hospital has a way of sticking to your skin.

"Yeah, Patty, you do seem strange," Lu added.

"Eight, seven, six, five . . ."

I turned to Sunny, trying to keep up my front. "Am I acting funny, Sunny?"

Sunny smiled at *funny, Sunny*.

"Switch! Down the middle!" Aaron now ordered.

"Funny?" Sunny asked, his noodle-y body bent over, hanging limp, his fingertips pressing the track. "Not funny. But yeah, kinda weird."

"Told you," Ghost said, low. I didn't know what it was about these guys. Except for Lu, I had only known them for a few weeks, and they could already tell when something was going on with me. I mean, I could always tell when something was wrong with them, because something was always wrong with them. But the fact that they could pick me apart so easily was crazy.

"Above your head!" Aaron called out.

"It's just that my—" I started to tell them, but Coach cut me off.

"Focus, newbies! We're not talking, we're stretching! It's been an eventful week, and you four always seemed to be part of the events. So today, keep your heads in the lane." Lu and Ghost had their arms up but tucked their chins, almost as if they were sniffing their pits, when really they were just sneak-looking at me. I gave them a *yes, something's going on and I'll tell you later* sort of nod.

After a few more stretches, and Aaron's way-too-serious countdowns, it was time to run.

"Okay, so we lost a day yesterday. And y'all know we gotta make up for it today," Coach said, spinning his car keys on his index finger. The whole team seemed to brace itself—we all knew what was coming. "So here's what's going to happen. Coach Whit is gonna lead y'all on the long run as usual. But it's going to be a little different. All of you who aren't running relays will run the regular way. But all my relay runners are going to stagger." Coach Whit stood off to the side, kicking her legs behind her, one at a time, catching them by the ankle and holding them for an extra quad stretch. That should've been a sign. If the coaches are doing extra stretches, we're in for a doozy. "What this means is, according to what leg you're running on Saturday, that's the order in which you run this long run. So, for the girls, Deja, you're gonna start off with everybody else. Same goes for you, Freddy. Stay with the pack. Now when they get about ninety seconds out, I'll blow the whistle and our second legs, Brit-Brat and Mikey, y'all will start. Your job is to keep a steady pace but

not to catch up with the rest of them. Understand?"
Brit-Brat nodded.

"Yeah," Mikey grumbled.

"Ninety seconds after them, Krystal and Eric,"
Coach said. I was happy he didn't call my name,
because everybody knows the third leg is the weakest.
"And then come our anchors." Coach held two fingers
out and pointed them at me and Curron. "That's you
two." Curron was known for false starts during his
individual eight hundreds, but apparently he was the
man as the anchor leg for the relay. And I gotta admit
that while today had been the pits so far, I couldn't
help but be a little gassed about the fact that I was chosen for the anchor.

Coach pulled a baton from one of his back pockets.
Then from his front pocket he pulled out a small jar of
Vaseline. He popped the top off, slathered the baton in
the petroleum jelly, and handed it to Curron. Gross! I
could tell Curron thought so too. Then Coach pulled
another baton out and gave it the same oily rubdown,
handing that one to me. Uuughhhh. "Patty, after the
other day, plus your temper tantrum last meet, I wasn't
sure. But I feel like you've got the heart for this. Like
you can handle this responsibility. I don't know why,
but I feel like you're the comeback kid. Prove me right,"

Coach said like a cornball before releasing the baton.

"Got you," I said, cool, switching hands, wiping the grease on my shorts.

Coach cleaned his hands on the towel that seemed to live around his neck, then raised his voice. "Listen up. Here's how this is gonna go, relay squad. Every time you all hear me hit the horn, the person with the baton has to run and catch the leg in front of them. Call out, 'Stick!' Whoever is receiving the baton cannot turn around—you have to find the rhythm of the run, reach back and take the baton, just like you went through on Tuesday. Then you continue running on pace until you hear my horn. Then the person with the baton has to catch the next leg and hand off the stick. At the end of the run, all first legs should have the baton, and you should all be together. You start apart, but you end together. Everyone needs to make sure of that. This is like a reverse relay, but it's good to push ourselves, especially since as relay runners, a lot of times it'll be your job to eat up track and make up time. If anyone messes up the handoff and drops the baton—I don't care that it's slippery—the relay team has to start the process over, meaning, if Mikey drops it, we start again with Curron. Got it?"

We all just sort of nodded, numbly. This was going to be hell.

"I don't understand nods and I can't read minds," Coach growled.

"We got it, Coach," Mikey said, putting on his game face.

"Yeah, Coach," Krystal said, game-faced too. "Pass and don't drop."

"Again, everyone is responsible for everyone. In relay, you win and lose as a team. You are not two legs, you are eight," Coach droned. "Now, the rest of you non-relayers, you know what this is. Ghost, I don't wanna see you in last. Lu, if Ghost is in last, you owe me a mile."

Lu's mouth dropped. "What?"

Coach ignored him and kept on preaching. "And, Sunny, if you don't finish first, you're gonna be running sprints."

"Got it, Coach," Sunny said, totally unflustered.

"The best never rest. Now let's get it."

"First legs and non-relays, follow me!" Whit said, taking off. Me, Krystal, Curron, Mikey, Brit-Brat, and Eric all hung back. Coach eyed his stopwatch and as soon as it hit ninety seconds, I guessed, he blew the whistle and Brit-Brat and Mikey took off. After another ninety seconds, the whistle blew again. Krystal and Eric headed out. Curron and I were last, holding our greasy batons, waiting for our whistle. Coach made his way to his taxi—the Motivation Mobile—had his arm out the window, the other holding the stopwatch. Then, *wheeeet!* And me and Curron broke out, off the track, through the grass and onto the street, seeing sets of two in front of us, and in the far distance the jostling mob of colorful cutoff T-shirts and jerseys, bush-balls and cornrows, and farthest ahead, Sunny, tall and light, towering above everyone.

"Just keep pace," Curron suggested, as we trotted down the street. "If you can."

"If I can?" I shot back. I was not in the mood for his mess.

Curron tried to back it up. "I mean, not because you're not fast, but because my legs are longer," he said, opening his stride. But he clearly had no idea who I was. Patina Jones. No junk. Frida in a suit. Mary J. Blige in track shoes.

"Uh-huh," I said, the baton glinting in the sun every time I lifted my right arm. I opened my stride too. And then, the horn.

"Let me see you push!" Coach shouted from his window as me and Curron started running faster. I needed to beat him, or to at least be with him. Didn't matter if his legs were longer. Did. Not. Matter. I got the legs of two people, me and my mother. We pounded down the street, gaining on Krystal and Eric, who had just reached a construction site. Workers in hard hats were hoisting big metal containers on ropes and hooks up to the roof of a building. Krystal and Eric cut into the street to get around the orange cones and yellow tape, and we would have to do the same. Thankfully, there wasn't much traffic.

Curron started to pull ahead, so I turned on the jets and really started burning my legs out, even though I knew it was a bad idea. But I was no way going to take another loss. Not today. I stepped off the sidewalk well before the construction and ran in the street, close to the curb to avoid an oncoming delivery van.

"Back on the sidewalk, Patty!" Coach yelled through his megaphone. I ignored him. "Patty. Back on the sidewalk!" A bus was coming up the block, the roaring of its engine like a bear waking from its sleep. *Coach is gonna kill me*, I thought, *but so what. Come on, Patty. You got this.* Almost at the construction. Curron was just a few steps behind me, still on the sidewalk, the *pit-pat* of his footsteps in my ear. Coach in my ear. The horn of the bus in my ear.

Come on. Come on, Patty. Krystal was close. I could see her ponytail flicking in the wind like a brown flame. Curron was gaining on me. But he had his work cut out for him, because Eric was farther ahead than Krystal. Now the bus was only a few yards away from me. *Honk! Honk!* "Patty!" Coach bellowed. The bus was right . . . there. I was at the construction site. Hard hats. Metal clanging. Men talking. Laughing. The bus was right in front of me. *Honnnnnnk!*

And I hopped back onto the curb at the last second, avoiding the bus and the construction site. Curron however, was stuck.

Keep pushin', Patty. Krystal was five feet away. Four. "Stick! Stick!" I yelled, just like we'd learned in practice. I took the inside of the sidewalk, running closer to the shop doors, while Krystal smoothly slid to the outside, skimming the curb. "Stick!" I pushed the word out, now gasping for air. Krystal stretched her arm behind her, speeding up as I was coming in fast. And just like dancing, like being able to move with each other without actually touching, in one smooth motion I handed the baton to Krystal.

And suddenly, I was winded. I fell back a bit, while Krystal kept her pace. Then came the second horn. And Krystal now had to catch Brit-Brat, who was, at this point, a speck in the distance. Ahead of her, scatterings of everyone else. Krystal pushed forward while

I stayed about fifteen steps behind her, passing Lu and Ghost, who'd pulled over on the sidewalk. Ghost was hunched over puking up purple. So it wasn't candy. Probably soda. Lu, standing over him, was yelling, "Come on, man! Hurry up and get it out so we can go!"

"Get it together, Ghost!" Coach barked on the infamous megaphone. Aaron was just ahead of us, looking over his shoulder, his bottom lip hanging.

In another minute it was Krystal's turn in the red zone, close enough to get the baton to Brit-Brat. I wasn't far behind, my heart beating so hard it felt like it was rocking side to side. Hard, like it was trying to pump the blood out of my body. "Stick!" Krystal yelled. And like with the last pass-off, Brit-Brat, with those big ol' feet of hers, sped up, just enough to fall right into rhythm with Krystal's stride. Krystal swiveled to the inside, Brit to the outside. Arm back. Arm out. Hand-off. Perfection. Just dancing the waltz. I fought back a grin. Whit's crazy waltz. Yeah.

Just about the time we expected to hear the third horn, we instead heard the clang of metal on concrete, like someone had rang a bell. A baton had been dropped, but not by any of the girls. We were holding tight, waiting on Coach to hit the horn again so Brit-Brat could catch Deja, and we could bring it home.

jason reynolds

"Start again, fellas!" Coach was yelling at the guys' relay. "Back to Curron. No dropping the stick! NO DROPPING THE STICK!" By the time Brit-Brat sailed over to Deja, she was done. All of us were. The final handoff was fine. Not perfect, but not terrible. And, hey, we killed the guys! But our legs were shot. And on top of all that, none of us knew where to go because Whit was gone, probably chasing after Sunny who runs long distance like it's a leisurely walk to his locker. The sweetest show-off ever.

"Where did they go?" Deja asked, slowing, waiting for the rest of us to catch up. We jogged in place on the corner trying to figure out where to head next. We knew better than to stop running. Coach was heading our way in the taxi; if he caught us standing, he would give us the blues. And the jazz. And the freakin' rock and roll. So we kept our legs moving. Like he said, the best never rest.

"What are you waiting for?" he called out, his taxi creeping up the street, emergency blinkers on.

"We don't know which way to go!" Krystal called out.

"We don't know where Whit went!" I added. Coach smirked.

"So?" he said, like this wasn't an issue.

"So what should we do?" I asked.

176

"You tell me." he replied. Now the guys relay team caught up to us, their mouths hanging open. I looked to the right. Hardware store. Man on the sidewalk selling used books. I looked to the left. An old woman sweeping the steps of a church. A little girl with a much smaller broom, helping. Her hair in dookie braids, maybe five or six of them sprouting every which way like antennae.

"This way," I decided, heading left toward the little girl. I didn't know if it was the right way, but in that moment, with Coach looking at me all crazy, I knew I had to do something. The comeback kid. Let's see if I could be the "get-back kid" and get us back to the park. Everyone followed as I led, until Coach finally pulled up beside us again.

"Follow me," he said, grinning out the window. He headed straight, which meant I was leading us in the right direction. Phew. And from there, Coach led the rest of the way back to the track.

When we arrived at the park, everyone crashed, rolling onto the track like cars whose tires had just blown out. And for once, Coach let us stay down there. He even brought our water bottles over to us! Sunny and Whit, on the other hand, were leaning against the fence having a casual conversation. They didn't even have the decency to be panting or nothing, while the rest of us were trying not to cry like babies. Ghost and Lu came sputtering in a little after us, Ghost dehydrated from all the puking, and Lu purposely jogging a few steps behind him, one hand on Ghost's back, almost pushing him along so that he wouldn't be last. Aaron immediately handed his water bottle to Ghost, who pretty much crushed whatever was left in it. I gave mine to Lu, who took a swig then gave it back.

"Good job, good job!" Coach said. "Give it up," he added, now clapping his hands. He went on. "Relay is about everyone pulling their weight. But sometimes, there has to be one person to just take over. Take the inside lane, and go for blood. Make a decision, because sometimes, there won't be a leader there to tell you. There won't be a coach or a frontrunner or a roadmap. Sometimes, you just gotta make a decision, take a turn and see what happens. If you trust yourself, nine times outta ten, you'll get to where you're supposed to be."

"Wish where we were supposed to be was down my street. Woulda went home," Lu mumbled. Ghost was on his knees trying to catch his breath. I would've laughed at what Lu said, but I didn't have the energy. None of us did. Plus, he said it a little too loud.

"No, see, that's where you want to be, son." Coach picked up the two batons from the track, and wiped them down. "But this is where you need to be." He slipped the metal sticks in his pockets. "And you know why, Lu?" Lu lifted his head, eyes on Coach. "Because you and Ghost owe me a mile."

"Coach, I was last! Not Ghost. You said, 'Ghost can't be last.'" Lu looked apoplectic.

"Yeah, but I don't ever want you to be okay with being last, son. So you both owe me one. Everybody else, I'll see y'all Saturday, bright and early. We're gonna try these relays, and if they look good, we'll start working on other ones, and maybe even some hurdles." The rest of us got up, limped our way to the benches. Car doors started slamming as parents showed up to pick up their half-dead kids. You could see others poking their heads out of the windows, trying to understand why the track looked like an apocalypse movie.

I looked for Momly, then caught myself, realizing that she wouldn't be there. Couldn't be. But there was Uncle Tony. He was holding Maddy by the shoulders—Maddy, unbroken, breathing—they both looked tired, as if they'd been running too. A rush of feelings came washing over me. The sizzle in my lungs now becoming a full fireball dropping into my gut. I turned back toward the track for a quick moment of *Get yourself together, Patty. Be strong, Patty.* I was looking out toward the track but not at the track. Not at anything.

I shook my head—refocus, girl!

"It ain't gotta be fast, but it's gotta be done," Coach was saying to Lu and Ghost, and as the blur cleared, I saw them both now standing with their hands resting on their heads, their breathing almost back to normal. But they looked pathetic. Exhausted. And they had to put in another mile. Poor guys.

Deja walked by me, heading toward her mom. "Good job, Patty," she said, tapping me on the back.

"Yeah, Patty," from Krystal. "You ain't no joke. Let's crush 'em on Saturday."

"That's definitely the plan," I said, now walking toward Maddy and Uncle Tony. I glanced back. Sunny was still on the track. Still leaning against the fence. His father hadn't come yet, which was weird. The stiff-suit dude was always on time.

When I reached Uncle Tony and Maddy, Maddy gave me her usual big hug, and whispered, "There's pizza in the SUV." I let go of her, nodded, then gave Uncle Tony a hug too. Just reached out and grabbed him. I told him I needed a few more minutes. Then to Maddy, I promised, "Ten, tops."

"Of course," Uncle Tony said. And I turned back toward the track to join my boys.

"So, I'm ready to tell y'all what's wrong," I said to them halfway around lap one. See, I told Coach that if Lu and Ghost had to run, then so did I. That as a newbie, we also have to win and lose together, hold each other up.

"Somebody's learned a lot this week, huh?" Coach teased. He had no idea what I was feeling. What I'd been going through. How could he?

"I'm in too, Coach," Sunny said, sauntering over.

"Look, we takin' it easy, Sunny," Ghost said testily. "It's all love, but don't be showin' off."

And no one did any showboating. And once we knocked down that first two hundred meters, I was ready to talk.

"Well, we ain't interested no more, Patty. We over it," Lu jabbed.

"My aunt's in the hospital. The one that takes care of me," I said flat-out, to shut his stupid mouth for once.

"Shoot," Lu said quick. "Patty . . . I was just jokin'."

"I know."

"She good?" Ghost asked.

"Yeah. Car accident. Broke her arm and she's

bruised up pretty bad. And she got a concussion. Crazy thing is my little sister was in the car with her, but, thankfully she came out okay." No one said anything. Just kinda let that whirl around us for a second. "But on top of that, well, I don't think I realized how much she actually be doing. Like, how much she takes care of. I mean . . . she takes care of my mother, for real. So now I gotta figure out how I'm gonna get my mom to the doctors and all that so she can get her blood cleaned. Plus, Momly's how I get to the track. It's just so much. Too much." I could feel myself getting choked up.

"Wow. That sucks." Lu said, as we rounded the second curve. He jogged closer.

"Yeah. A lot going on," I replied, with nothing on it. "Uncle Tony will probably ask Skunk to help out with some stuff since he ain't working."

"Who's Skunk?" Ghost asked.

"Cotton's big brother," I answered. Which makes him basically my big brother and practically Uncle Tony's little brother. Y'know, my uncle just be looking out for Skunk's knucklehead self. Keep him out of trouble.

"And who's Cotton?" Ghost followed.

"Patty's bestie," Lu panted.

I shook my head at him, like really? "Ghost, Cotton is really Lu's boo." Not really, but they liked each other. Which was disgusting.

"Oh, word?"

"Nope."

"Yep."

"We just cool."

"Don't deny my girl, Lu, or I'll leave you laid out across this track."

"Whatever."

"Whatever, whatever," Ghost cut in. "Patty, just put me on with them rich girls at your school."

"Tuh. Boy, please."

"What? You think they too good for me?" Ghost's voice toughened.

Lap three.

I thought of T-N-T. Taylor, TeeTee, this is Ghost. "Nah, not even. You're too good for them, Ghost. They ain't ready for you," I said, glancing over, catching a slick smile creeping across his face. Then I added, "Plus, they don't eat sunflower seeds."

"They don't eat sunflower seeds?!"

"They don't eat sunflower seeds?" Lu repeated.

"They don't eat sunflower seeds," I confirmed.

Sunny, oddly didn't weigh in on the sunflower seed

situation. So we all just jogged, the sound of eight feet moving in rhythm, slapping down on the track.

Last lap.

"Yo, so how long Mrs. Emily gonna be in the hospital?" Lu asked.

"The doctor said they doing surgery tomorrow morning. Hopefully she'll be home by Saturday."

"You still gon' make it to the meet?" Ghost asked.

"That's the thing. I'm gonna try my best, but I don't know yet. I wanna be there for her, y'know? Don't tell Coach, though. I don't want him to be disappointed. He gave me anchor."

"Wait, so you not gon' tell him?" Lu asked. "Patty!"

"I know! But I'm still trying to figure everything out. This all just happened this morning," I explained. "I'll text him tomorrow, latest. It's not like he can train another relayer in a day, anyway."

"You better," Lu warned.

Sunny sniffled. The first sound from him since we'd been running. I glanced over. He sniffled again as we came up on the last hundred meters.

"You good, Sunny?" I asked. He didn't respond. Just ran face forward, and kept running, sniffling the whole way. Once we crossed the finish line, he quick-quick dashed tears from his face so no one could see them. But I knew they were there. We all did. "What's wrong, man?" I shot a look to where Maddy and Uncle Tony were parked. Coach was talking to them and I groaned. I had a feeling my uncle had already told him about Momly.

Ghost put a hand on Sunny's shoulder. "Yeah, man, what's goin' on?"

"It's just . . ." Sunny started but got caught up. "Sorry." He took a deep breath, got himself together. "Sorry," he said again. "Just, thinking about your mother. It just got me, y'know?" he said, his voice shaky. His father was there now, parked in his fancy car, a newspaper parked in front of his face. I knew Sunny meant to say my aunt, but it wasn't no point in correcting him. I got it.

"Awwww, Sunny," I said, opening my arms. "She'll be fine." We hugged, and then Lu and Ghost, my boys, my YMBCs, came in for theirs, too.

TO DO: Eat pizza! (and . . . do some other things, but . . . pizza!)

I WENT TO bed that night with a belly full of pizza. It was the first night in ages I didn't have to police Maddy's plate. The first night we ate without Momly's tired face looking back at us. Without the smell of turkey wings mixed with the smell of clean. No white plates to put in the sink, because Uncle Tony had us eat on paper ones. It was the first night that me and Uncle Tony actually had to help Maddy with her homework. She had to practice for a spelling test. She wanted to know if the word Dr. Lancaster said, "concussed," had anything to do with bad words. Me and Uncle Tony laughed, told her it had to do with a concussion, then we had to tell her that neither of us knew exactly what a concussion was. It was the first night that I tried to make small talk at dinner. Momly was always good at starting conversations at the table, even if Uncle Tony was better at stealing them. He couldn't start them, though. And silent dinner was killing me, so I tried to.

"Y'know, the other day I got into it with this girl," I said, pulling another slice of pizza from the box. "At practice." Not sure where it came from. Probably just thinking about how good practice went with me and the girls today, and how sucky it went on Tuesday. I glanced at Maddy, and she was in full-blown cheese mode. It was like eating pizza clogged her ears. She would take a bite, then stare at the slice as if it was talking to her, telling her how delicious it was.

"What? Who?" Uncle Tony perked up, tightened his eyes. "Why?"

"Just this girl, Krystal. I didn't bother tellin' nobody about it because we squashed it," I explained. "But she called Momly my 'white mother' and I just, like . . . lost it."

Uncle Tony slurped the hot cheese, then set what was left of his slice down. Grabbed a napkin, cleaned the grease from his hands and mouth.

"That made you mad?" he asked. "I mean, I know Emily's not your mother, but did that girl saying you had a white mom really offend you?"

I chewed on crust. Chewed and chewed, thinking. Thinking about . . . everything. I swallowed, shook my head.

"Nah, not really. It wasn't that. I was more mad that she said it like she knew our family. Our situation." I glanced at Maddy again. She was nibbling like a rabbit, which meant she was now listening. Didn't matter. She needed to hear this part. "So I had to defend us. I had to defend Momly." Maddy looked at me. I looked at Uncle Tony. He nodded and picked his pizza back up.

"You know, Emily would've told you not to get into no mess with nobody over her. She would've said she doesn't need you to defend her, because she's the adult and it's her job to defend you."

"Yeah, I know. She probably would've got on the phone and snitched on me to Ma."

Uncle Tony snorted. "And what you think Bev woulda said?" He took another bite of his pizza.

I thought for a moment, ripping the crust in my hand open to pick the soft white bread out of the crunchy part. I glanced back up and shrugged, bread between my fingers like a pinch of cotton. "Probably woulda yelled at me."

"Concussed you out," Uncle Tony joked. "Just like she's gonna do me since I forgot to call her and tell her about everything that happened today."

I tossed the bread in my mouth, chewed. "Yeah, but then she probably would've told me she was proud of me."

To that, Uncle Tony didn't have a follow-up joke, like normal. That was a first. Instead he just said, "I'm proud of you too. Me, Emily, Bev, Ronnie, and little Waffle here"—Maddy bounced her eyebrows at me and flashed a joker-y grin—"we all are."

This was also the first night in a long time someone tucked me in. I don't mean actually tucked me in, but just came and checked on me. I always did it for Maddy, counting her beads, and toward the end of the week when there were fewer to count—and after the accident there were much fewer to count—I would make up all kinds of silly stories until she fell asleep. Lately, they've all been some weird spin-off about Frida. Other times, I would just sit on Maddy's bed and listen to her make up tales herself until she dozed. Crazy ones about what our mother's legs might be doing. Maybe they were dancing in Mexico. Maybe they were off kicking butt somewhere. "Who knows," Maddy would say. "Ma's legs ain't no junk."

Tonight, though, my uncle came and checked on me. This was after he'd finally spoken to my mother. After my mother talked to Maddy. After she talked to me. After she made my uncle put her on speakerphone so she could pray. After she asked my uncle to take her off speakerphone so she could tell him what she would've done if anything had happened to Maddy, and how dare he take all day to call her. After she asked for Momly's hospital room number. And after she told us she loved us. All of us.

Uncle Tony knocked on the door. I had just finished doing my Frida research for the night and was sitting at my desk, staring into the mirror, wrapping my hair—combing it around my head and pinning it in place before covering it in a scarf, a pretty silk one Ma gave me with stars all over it.

"Come in," I said, tying a knot in the fabric.

"Hey," Uncle Tony said. He was holding an empty plate and kissed me on top of my head, the image of the two of us in the mirror, obviously related. Uncle Tony set the plate on the desk.

"Hey," I said, getting up and climbing into bed. Uncle Tony took a seat on the chair.

"I just wanted to come say good night," he said. "And to let you know I called Skunk, and he's going to help us out with some stuff." He nodded, awkwardly, before finally just saying, "And . . . I wanted to check on you. How you doing with everything going on? School isn't your favorite place, Momly's going through what she's going through, track is stressful, I'm sure, and Maddy, I know can be a handful because she's got your mother in her." He smirked just for a second.

"I'm cool."

"Yeah?" He didn't seem surprised by my answer, but he leaned in anyway and asked, "You sure?" He looked at me like he could see that thing on my face that Becca saw. That I saw in hers. That look that says I got thoughts somewhere I can't get to. Under-thoughts.

But what was I supposed to say? I mean, I was fine because I had to be.

"Yeah, I'm sure, why?" I faked, but before he could call me on it, I changed the subject, which, when I think about it, might be one of my hidden talents. "What's the plate for?"

"Oh," Uncle Tony said as if he had forgotten about it. He reached behind his back and grabbed it, then sat right beside me. "Well . . . I was wondering if maybe you would have a cupcake with your uncle." He extended the plate to me. "Go on. Your ma won't know, and you better not tell Momly or Maddy on me." A wink and a grin.

I gave him a blank stare. Folded my arms across my chest.

"Go on," he nudged. "For me." I sighed, bit down on my lip, and pretended to pick up a cupcake. Held the invisible cupcake to my lips, took a bite.

"Good, right?" Uncle Tony said, doing the same, his eyes starting to water. "Strawberry." I kept my hand to my mouth, now covering it. *Keep it together. Come on, Patty. Keep it together.* But I couldn't. I couldn't help but think about my life without my little sister, without Momly. My life without my mother, or uncle. And even though I was grateful for all of them, I wondered how my life would be different if my dad had just . . . woke up. Why couldn't he have just woke up? If he was here, I could just be . . . regular. But I couldn't speak. Couldn't say nothing. So I just nodded at my uncle, who was now wiping tears from his own cheeks, and swallowed my pretend cupcake. And then, it all burst out of me. All those stupid tears I'd been cramming back finally broke loose. I cried me a flood.

The next morning I didn't send Ma a smiley-face text like I normally did. But that's because Uncle Tony took off work—something that never happened—so that he could fill in for Momly and take Ma to the hospital dialysis unit to get her blood cleaned. And because Momly was in the same hospital, I convinced Uncle Tony to take me and Maddy with him.

It was super early, like around six thirty in the morning, when we left the house and piled into Uncle Tony's SUV. There were papers all over the backseat, half-full cups of coffee in the cup holders, and a few french fries—hard yellow twigs—that must've been there forever on the passenger seat, wedged between the cushions. His SUV didn't smell like clean. It didn't have that nose-itchy scent that we were used to in Momly's car. It still smelled poisonous, but not the good kind.

When we pulled up in front of Ma's house, our other house, Maddy ran to the door like usual.

"Once, Maddy," I reminded her.

"I know!" she shot over her shoulder, pushing the doorbell. "Coming," Ma said through the wood. The sound of locks unlocking. Ma opened the door and pushed on the screen door, which I held open so Maddy could get her hug, which was extra-extra-long this morning. Then I gave Ma a kiss on the cheek and wheeled her out to the car. I mean . . . SUV. Uh-oh. I hadn't thought about the fact that Uncle Tony didn't drive a regular car. A car like Momly's. One that Ma could hoist herself into. So as I pulled up to the passenger side, Uncle Tony hopped out of the SUV and came around to help.

"Hey, Bev," he said, opening the passenger door.

"Hey, Toon," Ma said, looking up at him. She reached up, took a chunk of his arm between her fingers, and pinched.

"Ouch!" Uncle Tony yelped.

"That was for taking so long to call me yesterday!" Ma growled. "And by the way, you look terrible in the morning."

"You don't look so great yourself." He gave it right back, smirking.

"Yeah, but I got dirty blood. What's your excuse?" Ma grinned like—won! She has the best smile.

"My wife is in the hospital," Uncle Tony deadpanned. His face changed, and Ma knew that even though she was trying to lighten the situation, the joke was over.

"Sorry, Tony. I don't . . . I don't mean to be insensitive. I'm so sorry this had to happen to Emily, of all people."

"Nothing to be sorry for. It's just a concussion and a broken arm. But it could've been worse." Uncle Tony glanced at Maddy. Ma did too.

We had to go. No time for jokes, and no time for tears, because Ma had to get to dialysis, and we had to make sure we got to the hospital before Momly went into surgery.

First we had to get Ma in the SUV, and when I say we, I really mean Uncle Tony.

"Come on, let's get you up here," he said, lifting her from the chair like a baby. He set her in the seat the same way my dad used to do me. I gotta admit it was weird seeing Ma be lifted up. Be held like that. And he lifted her out of the SUV just as carefully when we got to the hospital. I'd already pulled her chair from the back and unfolded it, ready to roll.

"First stop, Emily's room," Ma commanded. But we made a pit stop in the dialysis unit first. It was a room with a bunch of people sitting around hooked up to machines. Some were missing a foot, or a leg, just like Ma. Others looked pretty regular. It was like a blood-cleaning club, complete with magazines and newspapers, but most people were looking up at a TV screen showing one of those early morning shows like *Good Morning America*. They had some lady on there demonstrating how to cut a pineapple into the shape of an owl.

"Shoot, by the time I do all that, I could've just ate the doggone fruit!" a woman wearing a blue hat was saying as we came farther into the room. Her silver hair was stuffed under it, wisps sticking out the sides like she was hiding an old cat up there. She noticed my mother. "Hey, Bev."

"Hey, Theresa." Then Ma spoke to everyone else in the room. "Hey, y'all. These my babies, Patty and Maddy."

Everyone did that weird whiny thing grown-ups do when they meet kids they've been hearing about. I'm surprised one of them didn't ask me how track was going. I knew they knew I ran. Both my mothers talk too much.

"And this my brother-in-law, Tony. Emily's husband." I learned then that the whiny thing isn't just for kids, but also for adults that adults had been hearing about. "Y'all know Emily's in here? She's upstairs. Got in a car accident yesterday."

"No," Theresa moaned, in shock.

"She's okay, she's okay," Uncle Tony said, doing the *calm down* hands. He gave my mother the *really?* face. That's the face you give people when you wanna say,

You really just gon' air my business out in the streets like that? Um . . . this is Beverly Jones. The queen of the air-out.

"She's okay, but she needs y'all's prayers anyway," Momly said. They all nodded, except for one old man who had nodded off. "Anyway, I'm gonna go up and see her right quick, and then I'll be back. Save my seat." The lady, Theresa, nodded and patted the seat next to hers.

When we got upstairs to Momly's room, Uncle Tony went in first.

"Good morning," he said softly.

"Hey, sweetie." Momly was sitting up, spooning clumps of oatmeal from a bowl. Uncle Tony gave her a smooch. "Who you got with you?" Maddy crept in. And me. "Oh, hey, sweeties." Then her voice quickly zipped from sweet to sour. "Tony, why aren't they in school?"

"Don't worry, they'll make it there. Even if I gotta roll 'em there myself," Ma said, rolling into the room, purposely making an entrance. *Beverly Jones. The queen of entrances.* She planned the whole thing in the elevator on the way up.

Momly laughed. "Hey, Bev." Ma wheeled up next to her bed. Grabbed her hand. The one connected to the unbroken arm.

"How you feeling, Em?"

"I'm fine. I'm fine."

"You ain't that fine if my knucklehead brother-in-law had to pick me up." Then she leaned in and said just loud enough for all of us to hear. "His SUV is filthy."

Momly closed-mouth laughed. "I know."

"Hey!" Uncle Tony squawked. "I mean . . . it got you here, didn't it?"

"Yep, it sure did get me here. It also got me a two-year-old stale french fry stuck to my butt." At this, Momly couldn't contain herself and let out a belly laugh. It was so loud that it caught me off guard. I don't know if I'd ever seen her laugh like that. She also seemed super rested. Just, like, chillin' in the hospital.

"Sounds like the morning is starting off on the right foot." Another man's voice came from the door. It was Dr. Lancaster. He came into the room, shook Uncle Tony's hand.

"Dr. Lancaster, this is Beverly Jones." Ma turned her chair, shook the doctor's hand.

"Nice to meet you, Mrs. Jones." Then he stood by the head of the bed.

"And how are you today, young lady?" he said to Momly.

"Hangin' in there. My head feels a little better, that's for sure."

The doctor nodded. "And you all?" he addressed me and Maddy.

"Good."

"Good."

"Great." He put his hands together. "So, Emily, I'm going to give you the rundown of what's going to happen. In a few minutes a young man named Terrence will arrive to transport you to the operating room. I will be there waiting along with two others, Dr. Morris and Dr. Fisk. Nice folks, talented surgeons. There will also be an anesthesiologist there, named Patricia." The doctor paused and pointed at me. "Patty, right?" I nodded. "Short for Patricia?"

"Patina." I was used to people doing that.

"Ah. Patina. That's a pretty name. Different."

"Thanks."

"Dr. Lancaster, can we make sure Patricia knocks me completely out?" Momly asked. "I don't want to feel anything."

Dr. Lancaster laughed. "That's the plan. And once you're out cold, which will take all of seven seconds, we'll get in there and fix you right up."

"And then she can come home?" Maddy asked, eager.

Dr. Lancaster squatted. "Not quite. We need to

watch her overnight to make sure there's no funny business. But I don't see why she can't go home tomorrow. How's that sound?"

Maddy nodded.

"Well, I'll be here to get you as soon as we get word," Uncle Tony said to Momly.

"Me too," I said.

Momly shot me down fast. "Oh no you won't. Because you have to run."

"I don't have—"

"You do," Momly insisted. "You're going to your track meet, where you should be. There's no use in you coming back up here worrying about me."

I looked at Ma for a bailout. But all she said was, "Don't look at me. You heard her."

"Track, huh?" Dr. Lancaster asked.

"Yeah, she's a fast one. Got them legs from me." Ma shined.

"Absolutely," Momly double-teamed.

"That's terrific," the doctor said. "My grandson is a runner. I've never seen him race, and honestly, he doesn't strike me as fast, but he tells me he runs, so . . ." Dr. Lancaster shrugged. Checked his watch. "Terrence should be here," he muttered, just as we heard a knock at the door. "And there he is." Dr.

Lancaster grinned. "The kid is like clockwork."

Terrence, who I just need to say was fifty times better than any boy on the Defenders team or at Barnaby Middle, or . . . ever, let Momly know it was time for me, Maddy, Uncle Tony, and Ma to say good-bye.

"Send us all a text when you make it out of surgery," I said, ironing the wrinkles out of my khaki skirt with my palms.

"A smiley face, just a little something," Ma suggested, followed by hugs, kisses, and of course, a prayer. (Ma told Terrence he'd better bow his head.) And then we were on our way back to the elevator, but to different floors: Momly to the operating room, and us to the dialysis unit—Uncle Tony would come back for Ma in three hours—and me and Maddy were back in Uncle Tony's dirt-mobile, headed to school.

At Chester, Uncle Tony walked us to the office to get our lateness excused, and then I wandered down the empty hall toward locker 172. I had already missed most of first period but grabbed my English book anyway. By the time I got to Mr. Winston's class, he was wrapping up his usual theatrics and a weeklong lesson, explaining the final stanza of the poem.

> *"When can their glory fade?*
> *O the wild charge they made!*
> *All the world wonder'd.*
> *Honour the charge they made,*
> *Honour the Light Brigade,*

"Noble six hundred," he recited, his voice breathy like he was having the most poetic asthma attack of all time. "Is that not beautiful?" Everyone just kinda stared at Mr. Winston, which to most folks would mean, *Leave us alone.* But not to teachers. To teachers, when no one looks interested, that means ask more questions. "Can anyone tell me what they think this means?" asked Mr. Winston now.

The whole class became mannequins, which is the standard move for *please don't call on me.* But for some reason, even though I was late to class, I was feeling bold. Funny thing is, even though I thought Mr. Winston was a weirdo, I actually kinda got this poem, mainly because of church. See, it was that one Bible verse—which is actually like reading one long poem—that Pastor Carter said all the time . . . alllll the time, "Yea, though I walk through the valley of the shadow of death, I will fear no evil." It was his go-to, and whenever he said it, the whole church bugged out. And this

Light Brigade poem started the same way—charging into the valley of death. So . . . yeah, I got it. Got it so much I even raised my hand.

"Patina," Mr. Winston called on me, surprised. I put my pen top in my mouth, chewed on it for a second, then answered.

"It's basically saying that their bravery should be honored. That they did what they had to do, and they did it together, even though it seemed almost impossible to win."

The bell rang.

"Exactly," Mr. Winston said over the clatter of chairs scraping the floor and backpacks zipping. "Now, onward to enjoy your weekends, my noble six hundred!"

In math I spent the entire time thinking about how Momly's arm was probably at an obtuse angle when it broke. Maybe 230 degrees. That's if it snapped backward, which made the most sense to me. I also thought about the 180-degree turn I was going to make as soon as I saw T-N-T. Let them know that I ain't gonna be buffing the floor by myself anymore. That I ain't no junk. The floor being the Frida assignment, of course. Maybe math actually was good for something. Somehow convincing yourself to stand up to hair flippers (and fake

flippers), understanding bone-breaking angles, and esti-
mating how long it would take to eat three (hundred)
tacos.

Lunchtime. Friday's menu: tacos. Pick your meat.
Chicken, beef, or shrimp. Pick your shell. Hard or
soft. Cheese, shredded or liquid. Lettuce, tomato, sour
cream, salsa. Three tacos, $4.25. Everybody's favorite.

I didn't do no lunchroom laps today. Instead I just
got my food and headed to the table where Becca and
Macy and Sasha and the others were sitting. The table
I'd been sitting at two days in a row, well, except for
yesterday. I slipped in next to Sasha, lifted one of my
tacos, and bit it in half.

"So what did I miss yesterday, Becca?" I asked. I
was prepping to deliver the blow, that I, Patina Jones,
was done being the Frida Leader. I was sick of it, and
I didn't put up with this on my track team, so I was
definitely not putting up with it at this school. TO
DO: put T-N-T on notice that the Frida Freebies were a
wrap. Dunzo. Becca, who was holding her taco like it
was a grenade about to explode hot sauce and lettuce,
widened her eyes.

"Oh, I was about to tell you. Ms. Lanford changed
the rules," she said. Sauce was dribbling out of the end
of the taco and onto her hand. Newbie!

"Changed the rules?"

"Yeah. She's not grading us all together anymore. We all are responsible for different parts of the project. That way it's fair, y'know?" Becca explained. She put down her taco and dabbed a napkin to her hand. "I think it's better this way." Then she flashed a sneaky grin. *Um . . . me too, Becca. Me too,* I thought. But there was something about that look on her face that made me want to thank her. Made me think she had something to do with it. Anyway, this was great news. And it made Friday even better, and I don't know if it was the combination of it all, or what, but I was suddenly feeling . . . I don't know. Like I had some kind of magical thing happening in me. This must be how Maddy felt all the time. Strong in a special way.

Once I got to history class, guess who spoke to me first. Guess. You get two chances, and one clue. They got almost the same name.

"Hi, Patty," Taylor said as I came into the room. Caught me off guard.

"Hey, Taylor." I didn't put no funk in it. Not even when TeeTee spoke. No need to be mean to them. Plus, I understood what it felt like to want to fit in. Or at least to feel like you "fit out." I don't know if I would've been fronting like them, but I get it.

"Welcome back, Miss Jones," Ms. Lanford said as I sat down. "I'm sure your group members will be happy to see you, especially since I've adjusted the rules."

"Becca told me." I tried to keep from grinning.

"Good. You will still have to give a group presentation, but now each of you will have to cover a specific part of the life of your subject. I got word that not everyone has been pulling their weight, so I wanted to make sure I'm giving fair grades."

I was psyched, I'm talking totally gassed about this. But once we got into our groups, I discovered the other girls had already chosen which parts they wanted. TeeTee chose Frida's love affair with Diego, no surprise there, though judging by Taylor's face, there had been some drama over that choice. Taylor, I guess because her first choice was taken, decided to go with Frida's death. Becca was going to talk about the art, which I would've loved to talk about since I was the one who had been doing so much research on it. But it was okay. Becca was . . . she was cool. So that left me to talk about Frida's childhood, which to be honest, I was fine with because I already knew so much about it, including the newest thing I'd learned the night before, that after Frida was diagnosed with polio, which messed up her right leg, giving her a limp, her father encouraged her to play sports—soccer, even wrestling—even though girls didn't really do that back then. He thought it would be good for her leg, but turned out what it was really good for was her confidence. And I kept think-ing about that, not just in class, but for the rest of the day—that that's kinda what running was to me. A way to shut people up. A way to . . . I guess, sometimes even shut myself up. Just turn it all off. Leave everything, all the hurting stuff, the unregular stuff that seemed so regular to me, in the dust.

TO DO: The family thing (beads, bedtime stories, and . . . back to turkey wings, of course)

MOMLY TEXTED ME a smiley face at almost the exact same time me and Maddy climbed into Uncle Tony's SUV after school. I knew she had planned it that way—Momly plans everything—to make sure I wouldn't be checking my phone in class when I heard the *ding*. I showed it to Maddy, and she smiled big-time.

"Hold that pose," I told her, and snapped a photo of her—head cocked, big gappy-mouthed cheese—and texted the photo back to Momly.

"Are we going to go see her tonight?" I asked Uncle Tony. "Especially since I don't have practice."

"Actually, I think it'd be better if you girls waited until tomorrow," Uncle Tony said, turning his blinker on so he could pull out into the street. He looked to the right and to the left, to the right and to the left again, being extra careful, waiting for the coast to be clear. "She's pretty spacey right now since she's on heavy-duty pain meds since it's the first day. When I spoke to her earlier, she was talking about putting beads on her fingernails."

"On her *fingernails*?" Maddy cried out.

"See what I mean? Painkillers can be a zonk; sometimes it's just best to give people a rest day."

"So tomorrow then?" Maddy pushed.

"Hmmm. I'm pretty sure she's going to come home tomorrow," he explained, finally turning.

"Can we go pick her up with you?" Maddy followed up, the *thump, thump* of her feet in my back.

"Well." Uncle Tony gave me a look. "Skunk's gonna do me a favor and take y'all to the track. Patty has to run." He looked at me to make sure that was okay, and I nodded to let him know that it was.

"But I don't." Maddy made her point clear.

"Don't you wanna see Patty race?" Uncle Tony asked.

"Yeah, but maybe we can pick Momly up first,"

Maddy pushed more. I reached back and gave her knee a squeeze.

"Maybe," Uncle Tony said. "The thing is, Patty's meet starts in the morning, and Momly's told me a million times that usually hospital discharge stuff takes a while, so people aren't usually released until early afternoon. That's the way it normally goes. Doctors drag their feet and take their sweet time." Maddy pouted in the back, while Uncle Tony took *his* sweet time driving us home.

That night I called my mother and asked her to help me make turkey wings. Yes . . . turkey wings. Uncle Tony had been married to Momly for forever and never knew how to cook much of nothing, which was ridiculous to me. He would've ordered takeout, but I just felt like we needed to have a real meal. Have something regular. A reminder that we were fine. Plus, I wanted to make sure I was ready to really help Momly when she came home, even though Uncle Tony kept saying he had it covered. I mean, don't get me wrong, the driving thing was all him, and lifting Ma up, and all that, but I was just doing my part. Teamwork. Ha! I almost said, *Team wing*, which I guess works too.

So I called Ma for a practice run, and she walked me through how to make turkey wings in a way that definitely wasn't Momly's way—Momly put hers in the oven, but Ma told me to put mine in a pan on the stove. I was scared they were going to taste like bacon, because that's how Ma had me cooking them—but they still tasted like turkey. Either way, Maddy and Uncle Tony devoured them, Uncle Tony, of course, being silly, eating his with a fork and knife like it was something fancy.

"Goor-met Tur-Kay Wangs," he kept saying, struggling trying to cut around the bones.

After dinner, Maddy and I did our nighttime routine. And because it was Friday—five days after I did her hair—it didn't take long.

"Okay, let me see." I fingered through her hair, counting each red plastic . . . cylinder? I guess they were kinda like cylinders. Math! "Looks like you have thirty beads left. You started with ninety."

"That's not bad!" Maddy whooped. And it actually wasn't, especially since it was such a crazy week. There'd actually been weeks when by Friday, Maddy would be beadless. I always figured during those weeks she was purposely taking the foil off the ends of her braids and shaking them out for fun. I had never confirmed it, but it seemed like something she'd do.

"Nope, pretty good!" I agreed, squished up beside

her in her tiny bed. Her room, so Maddy, full of weird-looking brown dolls with yarn hair and scary-movie eyes. She named them all Addison. Also a stuffed giraffe that was bigger than her, that Uncle Tony won for her at a carnival. She named him Giraddison. Of course. And taped to the walls were a whole bunch of pictures of our family. Some were photographs—Momly always went nuts with pictures, and Uncle Tony always went nuts with camera filters, and together they had the nerve to get cell phone pictures printed—and some were drawings. Crayon on construction paper of smiling pink mother, smiling brown mother with no legs, smiling little girl with big muscles and red circles all over her head, smiling man, and giant girl with shorts and jersey. That was me. But I wasn't smiling. I looked cool, but, weird, everyone else was smiling. Huh. Then there were pictures of legs. Just legs playing kickball, or legs holding hands, which I thought was kinda funny. But my favorite one was of me, Cotton, Maddy, and Momly, with Ma floating above us, just a head and torso, and above her, for some reason Maddy had scribbled, *Merry J Blyj*.

"I'm gonna tell you a story," Maddy said, fluffing her pillow. "It's a good-luck story, about a lady who almost lost her arm, but a girl saved it because she had thirty magic beads."

"Magic beads, huh?" I propped myself up on my elbow.

"Yep, they . . . they . . ." She was thinking of the next part. "When the girl runs around, the beads go *clickey-clickety-clickety* and that's like a magic spell that heals things. It's like a special hairstyle."

"And did the beads have to be a certain color for this spell to work?"

"Well . . ." Maddy smiled. And before she could even finish the story, I kissed her cheek and told her I loved her more than all the cupcakes in the world.

The next morning I startled awake, still in Maddy's bed, my body cramped, her face two inches from mine, her eyes wide open, willing my eyes open.

"Uncle Tony said Momly can come home at noon!" she blurted, way too early, and way too close to my face. Not even a good morning. Maddy might be a YMBC too.

"Okay," I said, groggy.

"So Skunk gonna take us to your meet, while Uncle Tony gets Momly."

"Okay." This was basically what Uncle Tony had

already prepped us for. No new information.

"You think he might bring Momly to the track after he picks her up?"

"Hmmm, not if she's in pain, Maddy. I doubt it." I hadn't really thought much about the pain Momly might be in. I mean, I know the medicine is probably pretty strong, but still.

"She's still gonna be in pain?" Maddy said, the tone of her voice diving into concern.

"I don't know. I hope not. I'm sure she'll be okay." Then I repeated the same things, this time to myself, in my own head, to convince myself Momly was all right.

I don't know. I hope not. I'm sure she'll be okay.

"But she might be in pain, right?" Maddy doubled down, like she always does.

I moaned, long and loud, like a train horn. "Maddy, I don't know. I'm still sleep." I rolled over and snatched the sheet over my head.

"But you not sleep because you talkin' to me," Maddy said.

And she was right, I wasn't sleep no more. But I also had to get my mind right for the meet. I took a shower, then sat down at my vanity desk to do my Flo Jos and hair. For my nails, I was going to paint different-color squiggles all over them. It's just part of my good-luck thing. And I could use a little of that. Plus, they made me feel fly. Like Flo Jo.

Now for my hair. Here's the thing: usually for the meets I either snatch it back into a ponytail, or I comb it straight and leave it out, also like Flo Jo. But today, after I was sure my nails were dry, I reached up and grabbed a chunk of hair, split it into thirds, and started braiding. Starting with the front, I worked the left side, then the right, and then after about thirty-five minutes all I had left was the back, which was always the hardest part to do myself.

"Maddy!" I yelled. She didn't come, so I yelled again. She was probably in the kitchen, eating breakfast and watching cartoons. Everybody left me alone on meet days because they knew I had my rituals—hair, nails, begging for Flo Jo to give me some of her magic from heaven. Oh man, I really am a YMBC. The sound of Maddy's feet came skittering toward my door. "You called me?" she asked, knowing full well that I called her.

"Yeah, come in," I said, combing my fingers through the patch of hair left on the back of my neck. Maddy opened the door, and her eyes went wide. My hair was braided up just like hers. "You like it?" I asked.

Maddy grinned. "Yeah." She came over to me, pinched the ends of a few of my plaits, then patted my edges as if she was touching up my baby hair. "You did a good job."

"Well, I'm glad you approve." I shook my head.

"But you missed a spot." Maddy noticed the unbraided bit in the back. "Unless that's the way you want it." She shrugged.

My face went flat.

"What? It might be a new style."

"It's not." I grabbed the comb off the desk and used the corner of it to pick through my kitchen—the back of my neck—again. "And I need you to braid it up for me."

"I can't braid."

"Yes, you can," I said, calling her bluff. I knew Maddy could braid because I taught her, and plus, she braided her dolls' hair all the time. Now, she wasn't very good, but she could get the job done.

"But not as good as you," she argued.

"Yeah, well, maybe I want a Maddy braid. Maybe that's my new style."

Maddy didn't look convinced. "You sure?" she asked, now running her own fingers through it.

"Waffle, if you don't braid my hair—"

"Okay, okay!" she said, focusing in. I watched her through the mirror, the tip of her tongue sticking out of her mouth, concentrating, weaving the hair slowly, trying her best not to mess up. Ten minutes later, "Finished."

I ran my hand back there. Three of the fattest, loosest braids I'd ever had.

"They're perfect," I said. Maddy crossed her arms across her chest, all cocky. All that. I laughed. "Now it's time for beads." I opened one of the desk drawers and pulled out the can.

"You putting beads on 'em?"

"Yep."

"What color?"

"Hmm." I pretended to be thinking. "I think I'm gonna go with red."

"Good choice."

"But I'm only gonna put thirty on there. That's it," I said, popping the top off the can.

"Only thirty?"

"Yeah, only thirty. Thirty red, good luck, magic beads. Just like you got."

TO DO: Nothing (but win)

I HADN'T REALLY thought about the fact that I wasn't going to have a parent at the track meet until the doorbell rang, and it was time to go. Before that, I was just focused on getting myself together. But now that Skunk had arrived, it hit me that when I looked out into the stands, Momly wouldn't be there. Uncle Tony wouldn't be there either.

But Maddy would. And when I opened the door, I found out Cotton surprised me by coming too! Cotton! I thought she was coming home from her cruise the next day, but she showed up a day early.

"I got *so* much tea to spill!" I said, throwing my arms around her. And instead of us immediately going in about everything, she whispered, "We'll talk later. There's somebody else here to see you."

I looked past Cotton, and there was a head full of tight curls poking out the passenger side window, a sly grin on her face. "You ready, Pancake?"

"Ma? What are you . . ." I was so surprised I could barely speak. I mean, she never came to my meets. Not because she didn't want to but because she was always so drained from the blood cleaning and Saturday was her only real recuperating day, and she needed to save up her energy for church on Sunday.

"Yeah, you ready, Pancake?" Cotton repeated.

"Shut up," I said, giving Cotton another hug. Then I ran over to give Ma a kiss on the cheek.

Uncle Tony came to the door with Maddy. Peered over at me standing at the passenger side of Skunk's car, my mother's face still out the window. "Bev? What a surprise!" he exclaimed. I shot my eyes at him: that goofy look on his face was a dead giveaway that he set this whole thing up. "What?" he said to me, his shoulders lifted to his ears. Then he waved me over so he could give me one. With his arms around me, he whispered in my ear, "I hope you've been practicing the Running Man, like I showed you." Then he released me and did a quick two-second dance that looked like he was being electrocuted.

I told him I hadn't been practicing that—how to look ridiculous—and as he walked me and Maddy (and Cotton) to the car, he assured me that we could work on it some more later that evening when Momly got back. Then Ma told Uncle Tony that even though she had to tell Skunk to turn his music down because "ain't nobody trying to go deaf with all that boom, boom, boom," at least his car was clean.

"And cleanliness is next to godliness," she plucked at Uncle Tony as he closed the back door after Maddy and me climbed in. Maddy had to sit on the hump, between me and Cotton, my duffel bag on my lap. These people. They were my constellation, or however Becca was saying it. The dots all connected.

"I know, Bev. I know." Uncle Tony bent down and looked through the passenger-side window, past Ma over to Skunk in the driver's seat. "You remember what I told you yesterday on the phone?"

"Yeah, I got it, Mr. Tony," Skunk said with that same annoyed voice that all of us get around naggy oldheads. "The speed limit."

"Not. One. Mile. Over it."

On the way to the park, Ma (who was sipping from a big cup of coffee) and Skunk talked about how Skunk was having a hard time finding a job, while Cotton and Maddy were doing their Maddy fo-faddy game. They were also yapping about how nice my hair looked, especially those three braids in the back.

"She looks so chic, like a throwback Serena Williams," Cotton said, trying to be funny, but Maddy didn't get the joke, and loves Serena Williams (who doesn't?), so she just whipped toward me and blurted out, "Yeah! You do look like a throwback Serena, Patty." Skunk and Ma paused their conversation and had a good laugh at that. But I ain't have time for all this jokey-jokey. I needed to get focused. Especially since Ma—Ma!—was going to see me run.

The park was teeming with parents and friends, runners and coaches. But I was going to do my best to block out all the noise on the outside, and all the noise on the inside. I was here for one reason. To win.

And so was Cotton.

"You think if I wink at Lu on the track, he'll wink back?" Cotton asked.

"What? Are you serious? I can't do this right now, Cotton." I said that, but of course I still did it. "You think Lu is gonna be able to see you wink?" I pulled Ma's wheelchair out of Skunk's trunk. Unfolded it. Maddy held my duffel bag and looked out at the track.

"Uh, Patty, have you seen these lashes? Yeah, I think he'll be able to see me wink."

"He won't. Trust me. When you're on the track, the only thing you're looking at are the runners around you, and the finish line. I mean, sometimes I can see family, but still. He might not even look up in your direction." I wheeled the chair to the side, while Ma balanced herself and slowly slid onto the seat.

"Well, even if he don't see it, he'll feel it and it'll still be good luck," Cotton said low so my mother wouldn't hear.

"Then wink at me, too."

"Patty, please. Maddy already told me you got all the good luck you need," she teased, flicking one of my beaded braids. "And don't forget, if you win, you gotta strut off the track like Mary." Cotton did a few power steps, MJB style.

"I got it, Pancake," Ma interjected as I tried to push her. "You get over there to your team."

"Ma, it's grass and other stuff over there. I'll push you."

"Patty, go. We here to support you. Not for you to

worry about us. I got Skunky here if I need help. Ain't that right?"

"Yeah, I got her, Patty." Skunk hit the alarm on his car. *Bloop-bloop!*

"So give me a hug." Ma spread her arms out. I leaned into her, pressed my lips to her cheek again. She whispered, "Remember, you ain't no junk." She grabbed my hands and it was like she whispered electricity into me, my insides fluttering in a weird way. I couldn't help but cheese. I couldn't help but stand up straighter, roll my shoulders back like Momly always be saying, and if she was here, she would've said it again. To walk like there's nothing on my back. No weight. And today, that's what I felt like. Then, and I didn't see this coming, Ma glanced down at my fingers. And then the glance became a stare. My nails! Uh-oh. And I snatched my hands from her with the quickness and tried to get going.

"Let's go, y'all," I said, scurrying and rallying Cotton and Maddy, taking my bag back from her. And as the three of us headed toward the park, Ma called out to me.

"Patina!" No. No. Please, not right now. Not today. Not here. Not before the race. I turned around, because if I didn't, it was only going to be worse. "I like your nails." She smiled wide, still rolled her eyes just a little, and wiggled her fingers in the air.

I threw my duffel back over my shoulder and we headed toward all the action, my face feeling like a bright star.

"Okay, Defenders, here we are, back on the battle-ground—" Coach was starting strong on his windup speech, when he glanced at me. I was sitting on my butt doing butterfly stretches with the rest of the team. "Nice hair, Patty. Different," he said, which of course caused a few giggles, the loudest coming from corny Curron. Whatever. "The lineup will be the same as it was last week, which means relays are up first." First? We were up first? My mind flashed to last week's meet. Not just the whole second-place thing, but also the fact that during the girls' 4x800 relay, one team dropped the baton. Yikes.

After stretching, we went over to the benches, got our last-minute jitters out by adjusting our jerseys and tightening the drawstrings on our shorts. I checked my nails. No chips yet even after fooling with that wheel-chair. Flo Jo perfect.

Mrs. Margo, Coach's wife, started handing out Gatorades. Lu's mom, who'd been talking to my mom, was now bopping over with a Tupperware full of orange slices. "Hey, everybody!" she sang out. She been doing this—the oranges—since me and Lu ran for the Sparks. Then she was holding the container out toward me. "Hey, Patty-Patty." Her voice only got scary-sounding when she was cheering for Lu. "Lu told me your auntie was in the hospital. Just talked to your mom about it. You know you can always come see me if you need to. I know you don't live as close anymore, but I'm still Mrs. Richardson. You and Cotton still my girls."

I nodded thanks and waved off the oranges. I can't eat oranges before a race. Too nervous.

But at least I wasn't *first* first. Boys' 4x800 was. Curron, Mikey, Eric, and Freddy took the track and the rest of us erupted in cheers. They huddled together for a quick talk, and then Freddy headed to the starting line. The other guys stood by the side of the track until their leg was up. I watched closely, my heart kicking as if I was already out there. Freddy stretched his arms over his head, did a few jumps, readying himself. The other runners around him were doing the same. Then . . .

On your mark, get set . . . *Bang!*

They were off, Freddy keeping pace with the pack. No one broke out on the first lap, but on the second,

Freddy and a kid from another team started to lead out. Mikey took his position on the starting line as Freddy rounded the final bend of the second lap and was about to take the straightaway. He was still neck and neck with the other kid. I glanced over at Coach, who had one finger in his mouth, gnawing on a nail. The red zone was coming up. The handoff.

Now people began shouting at the top of their lungs as Freddy came charging into the handoff zone and Mikey broke out. We couldn't hear him call "Stick!" but he must have because Mikey threw his arm back and two seconds later had the baton. The other teams did it the regular way, sort of, sidestepping and waiting for the runner to hand them the stick before taking off. Our coaches were right. This blind handoff would be the game changer.

By the time the other second legs got their batons, Mikey had taken the lead. And his handoff to Eric was just as smooth, as was Eric's to Curron, too. The other teams didn't stand a chance; our boys smoked everyone. After we all finished screaming and cheering, I looked down the line at Coach. His finger was out of his mouth, and he was nodding. He caught my eye. *You ready?* he mouthed. Then he waved me and the other three girls over.

"Next up, the girls' 4x800 meter relay," the announcer said over the loudspeaker.

"Y'all ready?" Coach this time asking all four of us. Whit, beside him, her hands behind her back, had a serious mug on her face. "This is rhythm, connection, and timing. Just like we practiced," she reminded us. "This is nothing but the waltz."

"Be there for each other," Coach added the last word, eye-lasering us.

We hit the track. The bleachers started stomping and cheering, each section for a different team or a different person. Me, Krystal, Brit-Brat, and Deja huddled up. "Let's show 'em how we dance, y'all," Krystal said, fierce. She looked at me and grinned. "Leave our legs on the track." Oh yeah.

"Wipe the floor with 'em. Together," I snarled.

Deja was up first. She didn't do any extra stretches. Just went out there, looked every other runner up and down, then took her place in lane three. She ran her tongue over her teeth like a wolf ready to feast. Slapped the baton against her leg a few times, then got set. And . . .

Bang!

Deja jumped out in front of everyone. Zipped from the third lane to the first in a matter of seconds.

Too fast. Too fast. Pace yourself, Deja. But Deja didn't slow up. By the time she hit the second lap, she had a pretty big lead on everyone . . . until the home stretch, when her legs turned to mush. You could literally see her downshifting from the fastest to the slowest.

"Come on, Deja! Come on!" we were calling out, Brit-Brat already in position for the handoff. As Deja fought her way into the red zone, Brit-Brat took off. Deja's face was a grimace—I could almost see her fighting through the cramps, taking one for the team, leaving her legs out there. She pushed through, screaming in pain as she handed the baton to Brit-Brat.

Deja collapsed, and Coach ran out onto the track to help her up. Brit-Brat, however, was able to hold on to what was left of the lead. She ran a steady race, her long ballerina legs graceful, which was ironic since she couldn't stop stepping on my toes during practice. Grace. Such grace. Until the red zone.

"Stick!" Brit-Brat shouted. Krystal had already taken off, and she thrust her arm back to receive the baton. Brit-Brat reached out to give it to her.

Except it slipped out of Brit's hand before it had Krystal's fingers around it.

Oh . . . God . . .

The sound of the metal cylinder clanging on the

track could be heard over the howls and groans of people who knew exactly what that sound meant. It seemed like everyone froze, everyone watching it bounce and roll. Really, nobody froze. Brit-Brat scrambled frantically to pick it up, like chasing down a rolling quarter. And once she finally did, Krystal, whose face looked like it was going to literally jump off . . . her face, and who had already run twenty meters, had to backtrack and meet Brit halfway to take the handoff. It was a fumble, and I slammed my hands together. No. *Noooo.*

This was it. We blew it. I shook my head and huffed, so mad that I could've untied my shoes and flung them into the stands. Forget it. But then Deja started going off. And I do mean OFF.

"GO! GOOOO!!!!" Deja screamed, snapping me back into the race. She had gotten up—she left her legs on the track, but now she was jumping and screaming. What was I doing? Coach told me, no matter what, I couldn't check out. I couldn't leave my team hanging. They needed me. Not just my legs. But my support. My energy. We needed each other. I looked behind me. Ghost and Lu were screaming their heads off. Curron, Aaron, and even Mikey were at the edge of the track, punching at the air with their fists, urging Krystal onward. Whit was biting her fist, while Coach stood next to her, arms across his chest, too cool, just watching.

"GOOOOO!!!" I belted out. I caught Brit-Brat out of the corner of my eye, covering her face as she came over to where we were. I grabbed her—snatched her right up—turned her around, and threw an arm over her shoulder. "It's okay. It's okay. We're still in it. We're still here!"

We kept screaming, but we'd already lost the lead. There were four people in front of us, but Krystal wasn't giving up. And neither would I.

As soon as she hit the back stretch on the second lap, I stepped onto the track. Rolled my neck, right to left, left to right. Stretched my arms behind me, clenched my hands to work out any shoulder and back kinks.

Lane three. I sized up the other girls who were taking their places beside me. Then I looked over and saw Ghost nodding at me and clapping. Sunny next to him doing the same thing. Lu had one of his arms flexed up, making a muscle. He slapped his bicep, then pointed at me. And Coach, still cool, was now looking at me, nodding. Like he knew something I ain't know. Or maybe, something that I actually did know.

You are strong enough. Your mother's legs. Patina Jones ain't no junk.

I glanced up at the crowd. At first everyone was a smear of color and sound. Except for a few people. Then a few came into focus. Cotton. I couldn't tell if she was winking or not, but she might've been. I could see Maddy, but even more, I could hear her, hear her screaming my name as if it was just her and me in a tunnel. And next to her, for the first time in forever, was Ma. Her arms raised high in the air, her fingers tickling the sky. I couldn't hear her, but I could see her lips forming a *P*. Pancake. She might've been saying Patty. But she had to be saying Pancake.

TO DO: Just run.

And win.

Here we go.

The other three girls had just made their handoffs when Krystal pounded into the red zone. I broke out and could tell that I was in lockstep with Krystal—in sync.

"Stick! Stick!" she yelled, and I reached my left arm back and grabbed the baton smooth as smooth. From her hand to mine—the energy protected, the power transferred. I opened my stride early to make up for lost time, and it wasn't long before I caught up to the pack, my beads clicking in time with my heartbeat. *Thump-thump-click! Thump-thump-click!* Long Ponytail was in lane two. Baldy in lane one. Twists in lane four.

Cannon to the right of me! Cannon to the left of me!

We all stayed together coming down the home stretch of the first lap. Now, for the second. Time to make my move. I opened my stride even more. Figured I'd make Long Ponytail, who was shorter than me, work for it. She couldn't hang, and two hundred meters into the lap, she rigged and fell back, as if her legs locked up on her and she had to pull up or something. Like she gave up.

The other two were still with me. Well, actually Baldy was leading Twists and me by a few steps. And as we came down the back stretch and hit that final two hundred, I felt my legs start to stiffen. No! It was like my muscles were turning into wood or something. No!!

Come on, Patty. Push. Push. Push. Breathe. Thump-thump-click!

"Come on, Patty," I said out loud.

"Come on, Patty!" I could hear Maddy screeching from the bleachers.

Thump-thump-click!

Final one hundred. The pain. The pain. The pain. Is nothing. You are strong enough. You got your mother's legs.

The three of us were neck and neck, shoulder to

shoulder, fighting until the end. The batons in our hands like broken sword handles. Warriors. The finish line. Right there. Leave your legs on the track. Heart pounding. Beads clicking in time with my steps, like a clock ticking in my ears.

Or a time bomb.

Come on, Patty. Come on!

➤ ➤ ➤

ACKNOWLEDGMENTS

As always, none of these books are possible without my wonderful editor, Caitlyn Dlouhy; my publisher, Justin Chanda; and my agent Elena Giovinazzo. I'd like to also extend a special thanks to Holly McGhee, who catalyzed this whole TRACK series. Thanks to my buddy, Mike Posey, for always being available if I have questions about the sport. To my family, friends, and former coaches who always seem to end up in my stories, thank you for the inspiration. Thank you to the booksellers, librarians, and teachers who continue to support me. I'm forever grateful to you all. And most importantly, to all the young ladies who feel forced to carry the load . . . this one's for you.

PATINA

BY
JASON REYNOLDS

Discussion Questions

1. Do you think Patty was right to be upset about coming in second in her first race with the Defenders? What does her response to the second-place finish reveal about her personality?

2. Why do Maddy and Patina need to live with Momly and Uncle Tony? How is life different than it was in her old house in Barnaby Terrace?

3. Why did Patty start running track? Toward the end of the book, she says that running helps her by giving her a way to "Leave everything, all the hurting stuff . . . in the dust." What activity helps you feel better when you are stressed or anxious?

4. Describe the relationship between Maddy and Patina. How does Maddy feel about her big sister? How can you tell? How does Patty feel about her little sister? Find a detail in the book that reveals something about the sisters' relationship.

5. Why did Patty change schools? How is her new school different from Barnaby Middle? What does she miss most about her old school? How would you describe your school? What do you like the best about it? What would you like to change?

6. How can you tell that Patty's mother loves and emotionally supports her even though she can't physically take care of her? How have the adults in your life shown you that they support you?

7. When they are assigned the history project on an important woman from the past, each member of Patty's group wants to choose a different person. Who does Patty suggest? Who does Becca suggest? If you were given this project, who would you want to research?

8. Why does Patty dislike group projects? Do you agree with her reasons? Why is it important to learn to work with a group? What does Patty learn about her classmates after working with them on the project?

9. When Patty is placed in a relay, she spends time learning how to be part of a team. How do her coaches teach the girls to work together? What do you think it means to be a good teammate?

10. Why is lunchtime challenging for Patty? Do you enjoy lunchtime and free time, or do you dread them? What could you do to make sure that nobody feels left out or lonely at your school?

11. When Patty moves in with Momly and Uncle Tony and changes schools, she is not as close to her best friend, Cotton. What specific things does she miss about spending time with Cotton? Who is your best friend? What do you enjoy doing with them?

12. What causes the fight between Krystal and Patty? What mistakes did each girl make? What strategies helped them resolve their disagreement?

13. In chapter 5, Patty, Lu, and Ghost laugh and tease one another after Coach makes them ballroom dance on the track. Why do the three friends accept this kind of behavior from one another? What might the reaction have been if Patty had said the same thing to kids who were not her close friends? Can you think of other instances in your life when you've said something to a friend that could have been interpreted differently if you'd said it to someone else? Why do you think friends are able to tease each other in a way that's funny, rather than hurtful?

14. Why do you think it is hard for Patty to tell people about her mom's illness and her father's death? What happens when she does talk about it? Have you ever held your feelings in? What happened?

15. What does Patty learn about Momly's childhood? How does this knowledge change her perception of Momly? How does it change her perception of her school?

16. Why is Patty surprised when she visits Becca's house? Why do you think Becca hides her love of

space from her classmates at school? Do you think she's pretending to be someone she isn't when she is at school?

17. Sometimes we don't really appreciate things until they are gone. What event helps Patty appreciate Momly? How does she show her appreciation?

18. Compare the race at the end of the novel to the race at the beginning. How has Patty grown and changed?

19. Jason Reynolds chooses to end the novel without letting the reader know the results of the race. Why do you think he ends his novel this way?

Guide prepared by Amy Jurskis, English Department Chair at Oxbridge Academy in Florida.

This guide has been provided by Simon & Schuster for classroom, library, and reading group use. It may be reproduced in its entirety or excerpted for these purposes.

TURN THE PAGE FOR A SNEAK PEEK
AT **SUNNY**.

Dear Diary,

It's been a while. And because you're back, because I brought you back (after spiraling your backbone back into place)—backity back back back—Aurelia, for some reason, feels like she needs to be introduced to you all over again. Like she don't know you. Like she don't remember you. But I do. So we don't have to shake hands and do the whole "my name is" thing. But Aurelia might need to do that. Today she asked me if I still call you Diary, or if I call you Journal now. Or maybe Notebook. I told her Diary. I've always called you that. Because I like Diary. Notebook, no. And Dear Journal doesn't really work the same. Doesn't do it for me. Dear Diary is better, not just because of the double *D* alliteration action, but also because Diary reminds me of the name Darryl, so at least I feel like I'm talking to an actual someone. And Darryl reminds me of the word "dairy," and "dairy" and "diary" are the same except for where *i* is. And I like dairy. At least milk. I can't drink a lot of it, which you know, because it makes my stomach feel like it's full of glue, which you also know. But I like it anyway. Because I'm weird. Which you definitely know. You know I like weird stuff. And everything about milk is weird. Even the word "milk," which I think probably sounds like what milk sounds like when you guzzle it. Milkmilkmilkmilkmilk. I should start over.

Dear Diary,

This is my start over.

Aurelia asked me how long it's been since I've spoken to you. I told her, a while. When I was a little kid and was all yelly-yelly and Darryl wanted me to be more hushy-hushy, he gave me you and told me to put the noise on your pages whenever I felt like I needed to, which was all the time except for when I was running or sleeping. Told me to fold it up in you, so he could get some peace. So he could have quiet for concentration when we picked at our puzzles after work. Yes, Diary, we still do puzzles together. It's still our way of, I guess, bonding. Anyway, after a while, my brain stopped pushing so much loud out of my mouth. Stopped noisey-ing up the puzzling. Thanks to you.

You know how a health bar makes you less hungry, but don't really make you full? Diary, that's what you are. A health bar. You take the hunger-growl out of my mind. And once I got to a place where the growl was pretty much a purr, I stopped writing in you. But now the volume on the growl is turning up again. And even though it's being turned up, I can feel it working its way down, pushing behind my eyes, and marching over my tongue, ready to come out. And my father, well, he still doesn't want to be disturbed. And I don't want to disturb him and his work, and his newspaper, and definitely not the puzzles, because the puzzles are our time. So, Diary, thanks for still being a friend. Something for me to bite down on. Something for me to whisper-scream to. Because sometimes I have too many screams up there. And they boing boing in my brain

      boing boing in my brain
      like a jumping bean,
          boing boing in my brain
      like a jumping bean
      my brain a moon bounce at a party
        nobody's invited to.

    And now I can put them in you, again.
    And now Aurelia's asking me about it. About you. Asking me about journaling. No. Diary-ing. Which sounds like diarrhea-ing. Which is sorta the same

thing. Aurelia told me she thinks it's a good thing I've been writing again. Even wanted to make sure I understood that whatever I write down don't have to make sense as long as it's really me. Really my brain and heart stuff. And that's a good thing, even though I already knew that, because making sense makes no sense to me. Sense should kinda already be made, right? It should already exist like love, or maybe sky. You don't have to create it or choreograph it or nothing like that. At least I don't think you do. So none of this has to make sense, it just has to make . . . me, me. I'm already me, but it has to make me . . . something. Make me quiet and calm, and maybe also make me brave enough to do what I'm going to have to do tomorrow at the track meet, which is probably not going to be quiet or calm. That's the real reason Aurelia's interested in you, Diary. She thinks I don't know that, but I know. I know because I know she knows I'm scared. That's why I brought you back. I'm so scared. And scared don't sound like eek. Or gasp. Scared sounds like glass. Shattering.

Scared sounds like glass shattering.

Diary, after all these years, you ever not want to be written in? On? Am I writing on you or in you? Or both? And how does that make you feel? I've never really asked you that. You ever just want to stay blank? Just be paper or whatever you think you are? Because I know what that's like. And tomorrow, my father will too.

Also, Aurelia called you a journal, but you're a diary, so I will call you by your name.